Syreen can travel for free — but she will also be the youngest, prettiest thing aboard. Aboard merchant ships, this usually implies the role of ship's cat, playgirl for the crew. As part of her covert mission, she must deal with this inconvenience.

She should also remain inconspicuous and invisible to the authorities, but without experience in covert missions, she's bound to fail. Can she achieve her goals anyway? What will happen to her if her enemies spot her?

Time of Worries
Copyright © 2020 Valerie J. Long
ISBN: 978-1-4874-2928-7
Cover art by Martine Jardin

Published by eXtasy Books Inc or
Devine Destinies, an imprint of eXtasy Books Inc

Look for us online at:
www.eXtasybooks.com or www.devinedestinies.com

TIME OF WORRIES
FORGOTTEN PEOPLE BOOK 2

BY

VALERIE J. LONG

DEDICATION

For all those who don't fear being different.

PART ONE—TRAVEL

CHAPTER ONE

When the first drop hit Syreen's face, she flinched and looked up for the leak.

However, she saw no broken tube, no air conditioner grid, no condenser — only a vast open space with a puffy lavender cover.

While she contemplated her next action, the ground around her filled with dark spots. She gazed about her. One-story buildings, side by side, with dark hollows where doors should be, with broken wires and empty mounts where once holo projectors had probably announced their venue's attractions, here and there with narrow elevated platforms to both sides of the door. They were sad witnesses of better times, when this backwater planet had attracted prospectors, traders, thugs, and the usual mix of entertainers, either addicted to their profession or desperate enough to ignore its drawbacks, like abuse, humiliation, and the loss of decency.

The condensation — *rain, it's called,* she corrected herself — intensified. The water mixed with the dust on the once even surface and formed a slippery grease that her worn-out boots struggled to cope with.

That's why it's called dirtside, she mused. *No way to walk more than a few steps without staining your clothes. Add broken plumbing and poor air conditioning. Many good reasons to feel unwelcome.*

Still, there was no point in speeding up. She'd be soaking wet at the end of her walk anyway, and slipping and falling in the mud wouldn't improve her looks.

At least she could already sense the intense emotions of a small crowd of people—booze-induced drowsiness, lecherous happiness, greed, and fear. There were more people, radiating hunger, affection, or disgust, but those remained in the background.

A few tencycles ago, I wouldn't have noticed. Not across such distance, at least. But now the beast is hungry, and it assists me in finding prey in every possible way.

The major advantage of this star system was its negligible space traffic control—at least, the local sensors were unable to detect a *living ship* pussyfooting into the system with its camouflage up, sneaking into the atmosphere and submerging in one of the many remote lakes.

There were no space stations nor any other orbital installations apart from a few sturdy long-life weather and communication satellites, so a stranger wouldn't attract attention just by appearing on the surface. There was no immigration or customs control, no ID check, no questions asked.

There was a spaceport for ships capable of going dirtside or for their shuttles, there was a small local force maintaining the pretense of law and order, and there was a merchant guild's office. That was what the database said, yet to be put to the test.

CHAPTER TWO

The rain drowned out the sound of jeers, whistles, calls, and music likewise, but the closer she approached the one venue that shed at least some light on the muddy road, the more noises she could tell apart.

The few words repeated over and over again gave her no riddles — *Take it off* in different dialects, pitches, and variations, but all close enough to the Common she knew. She could imagine what it was about, and when she finally reached the venue and entered, she found her suspicion confirmed — almost.

There was a man standing on a table in the large room's center who in that moment tore his shorts down and presented a remarkably large boner to the cheering crowd. A few of the women around pulled their shirts open to present him their assets, while the men instead turned their backs on him to present their asses.

"Shoot it," the crowd roared.

The stripper went on his knees and toward the edge of the table. Two women there picked up the cue and struggled for pole position — getting a chance to suck his cock. Meanwhile their subject of interest gazed over the crowd's heads, spotted the newcomer, and smiled.

Syreen looked down her body. Her soaking wet sleeveless shirt clung to her body, had turned transparent, and thus left little to imagination even in the venue's dim lighting, perhaps except for the process of ripping it off her.

She shrugged inwardly. No way to pretend decency.

So she reached down, pulled the shirt up over her head —which left her with only her boots and the skin-tight shorts, enticed a few whistles from the crowd, and let the stripper stare at her—wrung it dry, and put it on again. The fabric quickly soaked up some humidity from her body, but was no longer as transparent as before.

Her matter-of-fact performance disappointed and discouraged a few of the spectators and attracted some attention from a different group of visitors. She could sense respect, curiosity, and a more sincere kind of attraction, even if still paired with sexual connotations.

She granted the stripper a joyous smile and a sway of her hips while making her way to the back of the room. A few potential troublemakers with very straightforward intentions were easily distracted by a minor mental push.

CHAPTER THREE

To Syreen's amazement, the sounds of the crowd faded to a bearable level when she approached the counter. Who had designed the acoustics of this place?

Meandering between the tables, she collected approving smiles from people of both sexes, some clad in uniforms of merchant ships, some in multi-purpose protective suits with electronic as well as mechanical gear attached almost everywhere. She returned the smiles and dealt out friendly nods while evaluating her options.

That man. Judging by the number of stripes on his sleeve, he might be a merchant captain. He had a ship, and he could take her along — if she pushed the right buttons.

He was attracted by her looks as well as by her attitude, and she could also sense his protective instinct kicking in. Her skipper, daddy, and lover in one person? His looks were at least acceptable, his body in good shape — and healthy — his carotids were looking tasty, he smelled clean, so what more could a hungry, poor, lonesome girl be asking for?

She approached a free stool at the counter near him, pretending not to have noticed him yet.

He cleared his throat. "Erm, good evening, Lady. I'm Captain Estoril from the *Hispaniola.*"

Syreen paused and turned around. "Good evening, Captain Estoril. I'm Syreen. What can I do for you?"

"Erm — I saw you entering. The evening rain just set in, didn't it? Caught you by surprise."

"Yes, it did. It doesn't rain here often, does it?"

"In fact it does. Once the wet season starts, it pours. Every day, or better, every night, for the entire season. Which lasts a hectocycle on Klondike."

"Um. In that case, I was lucky to reach town today."

That caught his attention, as intended. "You came from the country?"

"Yes. A few tencycles walk from here." Her stomach rumbled—it couldn't have found a better timing if she had planned it.

He stepped back and scrutinized her appearance from her wet, messy hair to her still muddy boots. "Walk? On foot?"

"Yes."

Captain Estoril shook his head. "Sounds crazy."

Syreen shrugged. "It's not as if I had a choice in that."

"So?"

"No. Had to leave in a hurry. Either that or—" She drew a finger across her throat. Her stomach rumbled again.

Estoril's face showed concern. "You're hungry."

"Yes. I was unsure whether I could live off the country. I couldn't risk picking up a disease and becoming unable to walk on."

"I'm sorry." He waved at the barkeeper. "Today's special and a forwine." The merchant focused on her. "I had planned to invite you for a drink—may I now invite you for dinner? Please be my guest."

Syreen smiled. "I'm in no position to turn your offer down. Thank you very much. I'm infinitely grateful." She didn't have to voice that this included demonstrating her gratitude later. Both understood the implications of her situation well.

"Come to my table. I'll introduce you to my crew—" which implied a few more people to include in her gratitude—"and then you can tell me more about your adventure."

CHAPTER FOUR

The merchant skipper and his little crew of four hung on Syreen's every word. Neither of them bothered to stare at her tits anymore.

"I knew I had just this one chance to get away — briefly before the ship took off again, when they would no longer have time for a search. I slipped away and hid, and as soon as they were gone, I started running." She shrugged. "Running was not a good idea — too strenuous. I soon had to stop and regain my breath, and then I continued walking. I had a rough idea where to go — at night, there's some light around this place — but no clue how long it would take."

"I wonder what that's all about," a tall young man with short dark hair and blue eyes said. "Were they trying to avoid spaceport fees?"

"No." Captain Estoril's reply came quickly and firmly. Then he lowered his voice. "Don't play the fool, Roberto. Remember I once told you there are some questions that shouldn't be asked? Especially not in public?"

"Oh." Roberto ducked his head down and gazed at his mug.

"I know I'm not safe here," Syreen added. "I shouldn't talk about it. I shouldn't have told you — only, you were so kind to me, and — now I've spoiled it all. When they learn about me, they'll kill me."

The captain nodded. "I fear you're right. And I fear I can't help you there."

She put on her best puppy dog expression — she had

practiced that in preparation for this mission—and focused on him. "But you have a ship. Couldn't you take me along? I—I'll work off my passage."

He shook his head. "It's my policy not to take strangers aboard. I have a responsibility toward my crew, y'know? A pretty face and a pretty body isn't enough to trust you, even if I'd like to."

Syreen didn't avoid his gaze. "I know. I understand. I wouldn't do that either, were I in your position. However, perhaps you would consider making an exception for a *star angel* registered in the rolls?"

CHAPTER FIVE

Six faces were staring at Syreen. She could well understand the disbelief she felt from them. A star angel on Klondike, of all planets, was almost as unlikely as if she just had grown fangs — well, perhaps even less.

Captain Estoril was the first to find his voice again. "Where did you pick that up?"

"On Kyris, about eight kilocycles ago," she answered truthfully. "Captain Kasai of the *Light of Mandalay* registered me there."

He fought for words. "Why?"

"Well, let's say, I saved his ass back then — and those of his crew."

"You — you mean it?"

"I mean it. You can check with the guild, if they have an office here."

Estoril gazed past her. "They do, and I will check, as I must. But if what you say is the truth — which I no longer doubt — you're welcome aboard *Hispaniola*. My ship won't become the first to deny passage to a star angel."

"I will be grateful," Syreen promised. "And I'll work off my passage."

He seemed to blush a little — not easy to spot in the dim light — and she sensed his embarrassment.

"Uh, yes, that, well, seems a bit, uh, inappropriate. You — you're our guest."

"And that means I may not have sex with you?" Her frank question left him speechless again. "I mean, I can see that you all like my looks. The—my previous crew was less reluctant in this regard."

"Uh, yes—that's . . . that's why I thought you wouldn't . . ."

"No. I don't like being forced. I like being asked." She pointed at the table she had passed on her way in. "I like male attention when it's so nicely presented."

Had she overdone it? No. Three of the crew were radiating lust as only a one-track mind could, and she gently encouraged them to keep hold of that fantasy.

To be honest, she wasn't overly eager to copulate with them. None of them looked or behaved or smelled ugly, but that wasn't enough to consider a fuck. However, intercourse was always a good excuse for a little privacy—which provided her with a good opportunity to recover a little power, should she need it during her travel.

Be truthful, gal. You will need it soon. You gave too much, and that little outdoor walk didn't exactly help your reserves. Unless . . .

She saw the stripper—decently dressed again—disappear through a door in the back.

"Would you excuse me for a little comfort break?" she asked innocently.

Of course they would, and Syreen headed for that certain door. Her other *hunger* wasn't easily kept at bay right now, so she had to do something about it.

CHAPTER SIX

The sign on the door said *Staff only*. Syreen didn't care — she only instructed possible observers to ignore her until she had closed it.

Her target lingered in the first room to the right. She entered and closed that door behind her, too.

"Hey, what are you doing here?" the stripper asked. He was reclining in a comfy-looking chair with a glass of a light-brown liquid in his hand.

"I'm doing you," Syreen replied and removed her shirt. "You want me. I want you. Take off your pants."

"Hey, not so fast . . ." His voice trailed off when she pulled down her own pants and showed him her little black bush.

I should be able to seduce him without mind control.

She went on her knees, forced her way between his knees, and tore the front of his pants away. As in the show, the seams gave way as they were supposed to. His previously resting member started growing in response.

Syreen wasn't really experienced in fellatio — after all, what skills did a pretty girl need to wake up a cock? But she remembered how Herman had reacted to her first clean-licking, so she managed to make her victim's cock hard in no time at all.

"Oooh baby," was all he said. He tried a weak protest when she let his erection go, but when she shut his mouth with a kiss, took a seat on his tool and started riding him, he gave up.

This is how I want you. Hard inside me and devoted to my

demands. Now take your head back and to the side — yes, that way.

Next, she sunk her fangs into his carotid.

His lust, joining hers, almost overwhelmed her, and she had to struggle to keep her self-control, but firstly, she didn't want to share her own emotions with him, and secondly, she didn't want to suck him dry. *Only a little blood donation. You'll need a hearty dinner afterward, and you'll be fine. You'll only remember the sex, and how great it was, and each time you recall it, you'll have a boner for at least a quartercycle.*

Sadly, she didn't have a quartercycle right now, only the time for a comfort stop — only the time for a quickie, after which she allowed him to watch how she collected his cum from her pussy with one hand and then made a show of licking it from her fingers.

She put her shirt on again, stepped into her shorts, pulled them up, threw him a kiss, and left.

The beast inside her was satisfied, too, and she felt happy and strong, ready for whatever she'd face next on her crazy mission.

CHAPTER SEVEN

The planet quickly dropped out of sight below *Hispaniola's* crew shuttle. *Goodbye,* Assiduous, *goodbye, friends, watch out for each other while I'm gone. Grow back to your old strength. I'll try to find out what you'll need it for in the future.*

Yes, her mission was crazy. To travel to her enemies' home world, to infiltrate their lines, to sneak into their headquarters, to steal their strategic plans, all alone?

But *Assiduous,* her living ship, was too weak after his megacycles-long rest on a long-forgotten planet, and worse, had been damaged during their escape. He had to hide somewhere, had to regrow, while the Associated Planets' fleet searched every system in this galaxy for their lost enemy.

Raydancer, the corvette she had stolen during her escape from the AP's Duchy raid, was even less suitable for this kind of mission. Her transponder signature had to be in every AP ship computer by now, probably on the watch list of many civilized planets and probably even more lists of professional bounty hunters, together with her face.

That was why she had changed the latter with *Assiduous'* help. Not much, only enough to fool face recognition systems, but still startling her whenever she looked into a mirror—a habit she tried to get rid of.

Both ships, with *Raydancer* inside the living ship's cargo bay, were safely hidden in one of Klondike's many lakes, at least until *Assiduous* was whole again and ready to bathe in sunlight. That part of her story was true—she indeed had arrived on a ship that could fool the scanners of the merchant ships in orbit and even those of eventual escorts, had there been any. *Assiduous* was good enough for that. She indeed had walked several tencycles from that lake to the *city*, or what was left of it. And she had been terribly worn out, shaken up, torn down by the efforts she had invested to get her ship through a hyperjump without proper power supply.

Anything but seven-sigma jumps would have killed her. Even so, and even with *Raydancer's* power supply, each jump had been a walk on the razor's edge. But they had been forced to jump, had to leave the place where the Association had found them, had fought them and lost four warships, and would soon return with more firepower. So they had left.

According to their contract, she should have returned her passengers to Kyris. But after that last battle, the prospect of showing up anywhere in sight of an AP agent, being arrested and interrogated and locked away for the rest of their lives hadn't appealed to Drake and Crow. They had agreed to terminate their contract — and be hired by Duchy Fleet as *experts on antique technology.*

That way, they were entitled not just to keep an eye on *Assiduous,* but to examine the ship in every detail — as far as it allowed access — and learn what was there to learn about it. Together with Herman and Stephan, they stayed behind on Klondike until Syreen would return eventually.

If she could return eventually.

There were too many *Ifs* in her mission draft — too many unknown factors to even call it a plan.

"See it like this," she had told her crew. "As long as not even I know where I'm going next, nobody can predict my moves."

CHAPTER EIGHT

Syreen stared out of the small window next to her seat. Its existence told a story in itself — according to her instructors' tales, shuttle windows had gone out of fashion centennials ago in most star nations and in turn for most merchants. Her current ride had to be at least ten megacycles old. *Exaggerated . . . slightly.*

Ragged seat upholstery, rust-stained frames, blisters in the bulkhead paint, dust, and dirt added up to the image of a poorly maintained shuttle. However, she'd had a glimpse through the cockpit hatch before takeoff, and the pilot's place of work looked bright and tidy. The same seemed to apply to the engine — she couldn't sense any telltale vibrations or hear suspicious noises. Accordingly relaxed were her hosts — now crewmates — in the seats behind her.

Captain Estoril leaned over to Syreen across the aisle and said, "Would you like to join us on the bridge when we leave? I assume your last — erm — crew didn't let you watch."

"I'd be glad to, yes," she agreed. "Thank you."

Indeed she was curious to see what a merchant ship bridge looked like. Or in general, how a large ship's bridge looked, as neither her corvette nor her living ship could give her a clue.

A shadow fell over the window — the shuttle had entered *Hispaniola's* hangar. A moment later, there was a shudder and a metallic clang, and the motion stopped. This rough treatment didn't meet her standard, and her instructors would have frowned upon it, but it was still within generally acceptable limits.

Generally acceptable also were the quick decontamination handling and the early boarding, although she'd have taken more time after departing from a planet like Klondike.

The crew in the seats behind her left the shuttle first. She waited until the captain prompted her, "Your turn."

Syreen rose and walked down the aisle, stepped out of the hatch, and waited again.

Three uniformed persons were standing in a half-circle, holding tight to their little backpacks, and watching her. Wearing her shorts and shirt and with empty hands, she felt out of place.

The three men should be leering at her, but they only emanated respect, curiosity, and perhaps a hint of protective instinct. She felt more like their new pet than their new ship's cat.

Captain Estoril stepped out of the shuttle's airlock, followed by their pilot, and clapped his hands. "So. Welcome aboard our fine old *Hispaniola*, Angel."

"Uh — I . . ."

"Let me introduce my crew. Heath is our jockey. He'll fly anything, anywhere, anytime."

Heath was shorter than her, bald, and brawny. He smiled at her and admired her small tits.

"This one's Roberto, our cargo master. And Ross — our operator."

Except for the mustache, Ross looked like Roberto's twin brother.

"Chief Seb — he won't hear you if you call him Sebastian."

Seb was all smiles — in fact, if it was at all possible to smile with one's body, he managed. The result was a very broad smile, as Chief Seb was surely too rotund to fit into any tight places. But perhaps merchant haulers like this didn't have any tight places — except for the ship's cat's pussy, of course.

"So, these are all my crew members. Welcome aboard again, Angel."

Syreen decided to tolerate her new nickname, as Estoril was clearly determined to use it.

"Hello all," she said and waved to the group. "Thanks for taking me along. I'll try to help wherever I can."

As she could sense, they weren't entirely comfortable with the new situation yet, and neither was she. When she had sketched her approach, it had sounded like a good idea to offer herself to a merchant's crew for entertainment, but now there was no way back—did she really want to offer her body to everyone, anytime, like a puppet?

Not like a puppet. Not even like a whore, who would get paid. Like a sex slave, admit it. That's what you're doing here.

No, that wasn't true either. Nobody would do her if she wouldn't let them. She could even make them believe it had happened without actually letting them in. So if she had sex, it was because she wanted to. *Sex bait,* that was what she was.

Still, she had needed that little reassurance. There was a lot she still had to get used to—her new true self as well as the role she'd be playing.

She reached out with her senses—what was the role she'd be playing? Star angel, mascot, lucky charm? Ship's cat, wet and warm stress relief, snuggly cum receptable? Or—how had Teresa, Kasai's ship cat, put it—gofer, errand girl, dogsbody?

The first, for sure. The second—none of them would reject her if she made the advances. But there was some reservation she couldn't sort out yet. The third—didn't show up in their emotions.

"You might think that such a large ship offers plenty of room," the captain began. "But that's not true—most of the space is for cargo or aggregates. We have only little room for ourselves—the bridge, the workshop, the galley, the mess, and five crew cabins, including mine. Which brings up the question of where we find a place for you."

"I don't need much," she said. "A corner in the galley per-haps? Or—how large is your bunk, skipper?"

CHAPTER NINE

That was settled, then. The skipper's pet. Syreen followed her new master.

"You don't have to . . ." he began, once they had entered his cabin. It wasn't much larger than her own cabin aboard Raydancer had been — a desk, a chair, a hygiene unit, a comfortably large bed, wide enough for two people who got along well, and some space for his stuff.

She wouldn't compete for the latter. After all, she hadn't brought anything but herself and the clothes she wore.

Syreen approached her host, wrapped her arms around his neck, pressed her body against his, and gave him an elongated kiss. While he caught his breath, she whispered in his ear. "You want it, and you know it. Your body can't deny it." Indeed his cock was already growing toward her. She went on, "You'll feel good. I'll feel good. We all will feel good when our skipper's happy. Relax, and don't worry."

"I will feel guilty for taking advantage of your situation," he objected.

"There's no *situation*. You take me along because I'm a star angel. Every honorable merchant would do that. Now I took advantage of the fact that you feel attracted by my looks — don't deny that — and charmed my way into your bed. If you have to give up all your privacy for me, you might as well enjoy the advantages coming with it."

There was no way out for her, not if she wanted to stick to her role. And the pressure she already felt at her thigh made the necessary sacrifice appear much smaller in comparison.

"I . . . the crew will miss me on the bridge . . ."

"The crew will expect you to get acquainted with me and later guide your ship out of this port with a happy smile on your face. And they want to see that same happy smile on their star angel's face, too. So, tell me, skipper, how can we put that happy smile on our faces now?"

Chapter Ten

As the skipper had promised, Syreen was allowed on the bridge when they left the orbit above Klondike. After a look at the adjacent mess, she knew it was the ship's most spacious crew room. Equipped with large dashboards, big screens and bulky seats, it still looked like a museum to her. Where were the three-dimensional displays?

Everything around looked cheap, but sturdy. Perhaps that was what merchants needed more urgently than shiny high-tech gadgets.

While Captain Estoril headed for his own seat, prominently placed in the room's aft center, she became aware of a minor inconvenience — there was no seat left for her.

The skipper noticed her searching glance. "You probably should sit down at the wall over there — you can recline there when we jump."

"Recline?"

"It will become a bit uncomfortable. You've done jumps before, haven't you?"

She nodded.

"Good. How was your last jump?"

"I hardly noticed it." *Because it was another seven-sigma jump, but I can't tell you that.*

He raised one eyebrow. "Were you — uh — distracted or sedated?"

"Neither. It was an easy jump. Quiet, you know? It had to be — they didn't want to attract attention."

"Quiet?"

"Six-sigma."

Her statement made them all pause and look at her.

The skipper shook his head. "What do you know about that?"

"There were better times," she said and shrugged. "I've been a pilot. I did my own hyperjump calculations."

"So. You did." Estoril gazed at Heath. "How many?"

Syreen recapped her travels. "Oh, twenty or thirty. When they took my tac, I stopped worrying about that."

"What kind of jumps did you do? Standard routes?"

"A few. I also did a few shortcuts."

"Shortcuts?"

"Yes—for example, I found a two-jump route from Kyris to Brannock, without stopping at Skye."

"That's too risky. How could your skipper let you do that?"

She smiled. "I'd say she trusted me and my skills. I didn't disappoint her."

"Well, obviously you arrived . . . but in that case, you know how bad it can be. The route to Klondike from Appalahoo and back is bumpy, and not many ships dare to do these jumps. Four-sigma, you know?" He clapped his hands once. "Of course you know. How bad was your—*shortcut?*"

Time to let my pants down . . . again. "Seven-sigma. Both jumps."

Estoril stared at her. "Gal, you're kidding me."

She withstood his gaze. "Captain, I assure you, it's the truth. Put me to the test. Let me have a look at your hyper-jump data, and I promise you a six-sigma jump out of here. You can check my calculations."

"We don't have time for this."

"A quartercycle for me, another for you. Cheap investment for two sigma levels that will save you a fortune on engine maintenance—each time you return here."

"She may have a point, skipper," Chief Seb said. "Our old

lady here would surely profit."

"I want to see that," Heath added. *"Nobody* does a six-sigma jump in this region."

Because you're not a Navigator, *born to sense hyperspace, born to command a living ship. I checked the region on my way in. There are no obvious easy routes, but if you know where to look – if you* know *how to look . . .*

"Okay, okay," Estoril agreed. "Heath, show her our nav computer."

Syreen walked over to Heath, who eyed her with curiosity and a mix of contempt and respect while offering his chair to her. She brushed his arm with one hand. "I don't know this computer. How do you access it?"

Heath showed her, and she immediately understood why he couldn't have found a better solution yet – aside from the missing three-dimensional display, there was no easy way to list potential hypercorridors. The navigator had to know what he was looking for, had to enter the rough hypertrajectory, and the computer would show the result and offer minor adjustments.

Was there any way to display a kind of map, even if two-dimensional? The computer offered a list of available formats, none very promising. *Galactic sector star chart* – who'd want to check that? However, it was the only one offering a wider view.

"That's just the big map," Heath said. "Can be used for multi-stop route planning."

"Is it?" She had already called it up. The map spread across four of Heath's screens, pushing all the other panels aside, and offered a star chart with an outside look from three different angles plus a forward-facing view. Their current origin and destination as well as their hypervector were already marked.

In a way, it was similar to a display she had seen in her courses. *If all your stuff breaks up, you can still chart a jump on a notepad — in theory,* her instructor had said. *This emergency panel is the closest you might ever get to a notepad. It can help you adjust your memorized jumps.*

If this chart was meant to serve the same purposes, it should have — *here.* She found a zoom control and reduced the chart to the area between Klondike and Appalahoo. Next she found an option to add known and tested hypercorridors.

"Hey, I've never seen that!" Excited, Heath leaned closer and watched her fingers run across the controls.

Syreen added charted hyperflight obstacles to the display, then star classifications and potency gradients.

"That's a mess," Heath objected.

Syreen could only agree. This way to display the data was crude, messy, and hardly helpful — unless the user knew what to look for, and she did. She pointed at the forward-facing display with one hand and at one of the side screens with the other.

"Look here. There are multiple high-density zones that almost overlap. No way to get through there. But here's a less barred area, where your hypercorridor passes through, and with a little care to detail you can almost do a five-sigma jump. It depends a lot on where you jump from within this system. Currently the region behind the sun is favorable — but we're running away from that. As a consequence, the jump will be bumpy, probably like always at this time of the season. Right?"

"Uh — yeah, indeed. Wet season jumps aren't nice."

"But see this." She added some coordinates, and the computer added a different corridor. "There are a few close obstacles you must take care of, but once you're past them, there's a lot of leeway with very favorable gradients. Even this computer will need little effort for the fine adjustment, and the best — it will work from any point in this system."

She waited until Heath had examined the relevant data.

"May I?" he asked, and she vacated his chair.

Now his fingers entered a few commands, which she recognized as transfer to the navigation computer. A moment later, the star chart faded into the background, and his main screen showed a hyperjump data set.

Heath turned to their captain. "Six-sigma, skipper. No doubt, that's a better jump."

Estoril's gaze moved back and forth between them. "You sure, Heath?"

"I'll redo the fine adjustment when we reach jump speed, but yeah, I'm confident. Now that I've seen it, I won't recommend the old jump, skipper."

"Honestly, Heath. Could you have done it yourself?"

The pilot smiled and glanced at her. She could sense only admiration, no envy.

"Yes and no, skipper. Yes, if I had known what to look for, I could have found that jump myself — I could do it again from here, should we lose the coordinate set. No, as in fact I didn't know what to look for. I didn't know that you can use that star chart for such purposes, that you can zoom in and add all the parameters needed. I wouldn't have known that with just those few parameters you can create a comprehensive map for hypercorridor search. And even if I had known, I'd have been lost in that messy display. I wouldn't have seen it, although it's there for everyone. Another tencycle, another system, I'll try that trick again, but it may take me hectocycles to examine the chart and come up with something worth a try."

Estoril nodded. "Thank you, Heath. So it's not some mystic trick but in fact a lucky hit by our angel, right?"

"I wouldn't call it a lucky hit, skipper," Heath disagreed. "You know, each time Seb says the engine's sick and heads off in a certain direction, he knows he'll find something. You don't call that a lucky hit — Seb knows his ways with this ship. I say she knows her ways with hyperjumps. Let me watch and learn."

25

"What's your view on this, Angel?"

"Heath's right. I have a knack with navigation. Let's say that's the way star angels travel, okay?"

CHAPTER ELEVEN

Syreen heard approaching steps, sensed amusement and appreciation and heard a harrumph. She looked over her shoulder and saw Chief Seb in the door to the mess. With her knees and hands on the floor, she offered him an excellent view on her buttocks, only covered by her tight shorts and her bare feet, so she understood his emotions.

"What are you doing there?" the chief asked.

"What does it look like? I'm cleaning the floor."

"Our robot does that. Or did it break? I received no notice?"

"Your robot works fine," she said, turned around and rose. "Within its limitations. It's supposed to do a quick run each tencycle, a thorough run each hectocycle, and a supported run each kilocycle. The way the floor looks—and feels, if you go barefoot—there hasn't been a supported run for ages."

He gazed at her with wide open eyes. "The supported run should work as scheduled. I don't know of any failures."

She grinned. "I'm sure the robot does it—but what about the supporters?"

"Supporters?"

"That's why it's called *supported* run—because it requires human aid with those stains that the robot can't clean alone. So whose job is the support?"

"Uh—well—that would be . . . I don't know."

"See? So I decided it's my job now."

"But why? You're our guest."

"I promised I'd work for my passage. And what else

should I do while the rest of the crew is busy?"

"Uh, yes, but it doesn't feel right. You already did so much for us. My engines were never as happy after a jump as now."

"Fine. Let's see how happy your robot will be after the next run. Or how happy you will be after lunch."

"Lunch? Why?"

"I cleaned the galley first, inside and out."

"Inside — are you qualified to maintain galley appliances?"

Duchy Fleet officers had to take care of their own equipment — only stuff like drive aggregates, ordnance, and shields required maintenance specialists. But Fleet lieutenants weren't expected to call for maintenance just for a broken cleaner or espresso machine. Only Syreen wouldn't tell Seb anything of the Duchy or Fleet. So she just said, "I am."

CHAPTER TWELVE

Syreen blinked twice, and the slight dizziness was gone.

Captain Estoril turned around in his chair and spread his hands. "You did it again."

"Heath did it," she disagreed.

"You showed him. No, don't argue. I know Heath is a good pilot. He won't forget what you showed him, and I'm sure he'll try make good use of it—for our joint profit. But for now—Seb, how's she doing?"

The chief engineer checked his board, patted it and turned around. "Like new, skipper. I'll check the usual suspects anyway, but I'd expect no surprises. May I propose—"

The skipper waved a hand. "Yes, you'll have budget. Make a list of what you need." He turned to Syreen. "Angel, this is the first run to Klondike ever that will make a significant profit. Until now, even only the most urgent repairs ate up everything we made from the trip. Now we can afford some long overdue maintenance and get our old lady back in shape—and still have a little premium for everyone. What, boys?"

The other men cheered.

"The best is—we're the only ones who can do that. We're able to charge less for the goods and still make a good profit." He smiled. "You may ask why we did it at all."

"I was a bit curious, yes."

"Well, for one, there aren't many ships daring to take the trip. Four-sigma make every skipper think twice. And yet, we can't let the people on Klondike down, can we? At least not

29

as long as they're willing to pay good credits. For two, while four-sigma jumps are a strain on every ship, our good old *Hispaniola* can take some. A lot of discrete wiring, you know? Seb can repair stuff inflight that other, modern ships need a wharf for. We can risk the occasional glitch without stranding. Not many can do that. For three—well, let's skip that. We must be grateful. You more than repaid your fare. And that's why we'll share our premium with you. We won't let you leave us broke with nothing but the clothes you're wearing, okay?"

And this from a merchant? Syreen started to really like the old man.

"Thank you," she said. "It was a pleasant trip with you all."

That enticed a few smiles and the occasional gaze to her red, scratched knees.

"And now you must leave," Estoril added. "Because we're going back to Klondike, and you aren't. You should eventually be able to find another ship to take you along. In case someone asks, we'll recommend you."

"Just don't tell them I'm a good cleaner."

They all laughed.

The skipper focused on her. "Don't worry. We won't. We also won't advertise your navigation skills—it's up to you to offer them or not."

So anyone seeing me and not knowing about my cleaning and navigation skills will draw his own conclusions why I'm recommended.

Syreen suppressed a frown and grinned. It wasn't their fault that space travel was the way it was.

They still had a few cycles of travel ahead before they'd reach the orbit above Appalahoo. Again, there was no space station, so they'd go down by shuttle.

CHAPTER THIRTEEN

The moment she stepped from the shuttle ramp and almost lost her footing in the muddy soil, Syreen decided that she liked Appalahoo even less than Klondike.

Heath caught her by the arm and steadied her. "Don't bother to buy new boots. Or at least don't wear them until you leave."

"Thanks."

Together, they approached an elongated one-story building. One sign read *Appalahoo Port Authority*, another *Customs and Immigration*, and a third advertised *Cold Drinks and Convenience*. The steel doors below the signs were linked by a roof-covered boardwalk.

The few small windows were trellised. As far as she remembered, dirtside windows served three main purposes — allowing one to see what happened outside, venting, and lighting. The latter wouldn't work well here.

The same tall greenish structures that rose behind the building surrounded the entire spaceport. From peeking out of the shuttle window, she knew that these *trees* — as the skipper had called them — covered almost all of this planet's only land mass. She hadn't spotted cities or other large man-made structures, not even transportation lines, and from *Hispaniola's* library she knew there weren't supposed to be any.

Appalahoo's riches were the mostly untouched uninhabited forests and the likewise lonesome ocean that surrounded the forest continent and covered eighty percent of the planet's surface. Aside from that, it was a major traffic and trade node in this part of the galaxy — whatever *major* meant in this context.

"If you exchange cargo here — where's the space for it?"

Roberto, marching ahead, helped. "Underground. There's a large freight door in the spacefield center. Not easy to spot when it's closed — it's as muddy there as here."

"Thanks."

Captain Estoril paused to let her catch up. "I'm worried that there are no other shuttles. It's unusually deserted. Be cautious."

"Anything specific?"

"Everything."

She sensed a hint of guilt in him, and decided not to press the subject. Instead, she fell behind.

Had Syreen been wondering where Estoril was heading — between the signs for *Customs* and *Cold Drinks* — she soon understood the rationale when he reached the boardwalk and turned toward the port authority. The mud along that part of the boardwalk seemed to be much deeper than where they had reached dry ground.

"They make good money on boots," Heath commented with a grin. "Especially from new visitors."

"Shut up, Heath," the skipper said.

She could already sense the reason. There was no way to tell the originators yet, but the entire building seemed to radiate greed, malice and arrogance. Those people surely weren't easy to deal with even without joking about them.

SitOps. Situation — I can't rely on the captain and his crew. Even if they were willing to help, they must stay on the locals' good side, as they will return here and I probably won't. So I'm on my own with the locals. I can't entirely avoid them, as I must contact other skippers, and I can do that only here.

Options — One, I can try to talk my way through the events. However, if they're not open for talk, my situation will go down the drain in no time. I'm not at all inclined to be the port whore even temporarily. Two, I can use my powers to change their minds. That might require some effort – and once I run out of power, I have to feed on them. Which is even harder to hide. Plus, would I want to turn the beast loose? Three, I can sneak in and make them mostly ignore me. That costs me less. Four, I can stay outside and live off the country. Basic survival training for Duchy commissioned officers, second season – habitable alien planets. Have your gun ready. Oh yeah. What are the strong doors for, or better – what are they against? Am I ready to take that chance?

Option three would be a good fallback position for number four, if the planet turned out to be more dangerous than she could handle. However, how dangerous could it be if people came here for its scenery?

Syreen waited outside until Captain Estoril had finished his business with the port authorities. Among other things, he asked about recent visits and learned that his freight was already waiting for him to pick up – at a slightly increased storage fee. The clerk was quite disappointed when he learned that Estoril could easily afford the difference – and wouldn't buy as many spare parts as before.

She decided to give the clerk a little time to get over it, and then she moved inside. The overweight man made a point of ignoring her and scrutinized his panel. So he hadn't even registered her looks yet, and that suited her.

You're not interested in me. You want to call it a day. I can pass.

He waved his hand. "You can pass."

You're not interested.

She walked out and found herself in a windowless corridor paralleling the boardwalk, only stuffy and dimly lit. The outside signs were repeated here, and complemented by more labels for the inside doors – *Accommodation, Guides and Transportation, Backcountry and Hunting Permits.* Hunting? Did that mean people came here to kill local wildlife?

Such behavior was considered barbaric in the Duchy, but then the Duchy's spaceports weren't muddy, either. And with the beast inside her, who was she to judge?

She walked past the signs. Surely a local guide would be a good information source, but why would a guide bother to linger in his office when the only ship in orbit was a freighter? Its crew would eventually look for *Cold Drinks and Convenience,* so that was the place of choice for everyone.

The door from the corridor was wide open, and she heard shuffling noises from inside. She entered a large room with long rows of ceiling-high shelves to her right and five round tables before a long counter to her left. The shuffling noises originated from the only person in the room — a tall man with a crown of white hair surrounding a large bald patch and a similarly white beard, and he was carrying glassware around behind the counter.

He had already noticed her and waved her closer with a friendly smile, accompanied by some less friendly but rather lecherous emotions. "Welcome, young lady. Newly arrived, I assume. You're my first customer today — if you allow — so your first drink is on the house. What ship?"

Syreen climbed a stool. "I arrived with the *Hispaniola.*"

He leaned forward on the counter. "Ah, the Klondike runner. Tough journey, daring team. You're a new hire?"

"Passenger."

His face resembled the mix of emotions she sensed — disbelief, amazement, curiosity, caution. "I didn't expect them to be so desperate."

"For taking a stranger along? They wouldn't. But a star angel is welcome aboard any merchant."

That made him pause. He scratched his beard. "A star angel. That's a rare honor."

"I'm registered with the guild — they don't operate a guild hall here, or do they?"

"Nay. I take care of the rolls. So I'd find you there?" He snapped his fingers and started to wipe and type on the screen that hovered above the counter before him.

"I'm Syreen, registered on Kyris."

"Kyris, eh? Far from here."

"Yes."

He tried to stare into her. "Must be an interesting story that got you here."

"Maybe one day I'll be willing to tell it. This is not the time nor the place." *You don't want to insist.* "A cold beer, please. Where is everybody?"

"Every who?"

She waved behind her. "The locals. Shopkeeper, customs officer, guides, or who else lives here."

"Oh, the locals." He stood up straight, fetched a glass, and began to fill it. "Meet the bartender, shopkeeper, hotel boss, room maid, all in one. The officials probably all try to get a piece of the cake in the storage."

"Storage?"

He pointed out and down. "Under the surface. Freight and parts all go there. Skippers always need parts — most of all those coming from Klondike and beyond. So they must shop — from Port and Customs."

"But not from you."

"Nay. They're the ones setting the fees — for storage and customs. We have an agreement. I won't interfere with their business, and I may run mine — that is, all that requires foot-work. They wouldn't want to do it themselves, they need another to do it, so I could get in."

"Sounds like it's just the three of you."

"Oh — no, no, they just have taken their hired muscle along. Here." He set the glass down before her.

"Thanks. What about the guides?" She tried the drink. It was cold and refreshing, but otherwise no match for the ones she had sampled on Kyris.

"Guides." He laughed. "The *guides,* hah! They'll come in when the season starts, together with those rich brats who make the rules as they like it."

"You don't think much of the guides."

"No." The bartender leaned forward, down on his elbows, until their noses were just a few fingers apart. She could smell his breath, and might have been able to count his lashes — but she wouldn't evade this intense eye contact. "They don't know nothing of this planet, not even those who were here before. They're never here off-season. They have no clue. They come with their high-tech sensors and guns and armor and think they're in control of the situation, but they're not. You see the grates across the windows? See the steel doors? Yeah, but you don't see the armor beneath, hidden in our strong walls for the day. Put there for a reason. 'Cause, what's out there during the season, all the fierce, wild creatures they're hunting for trophies, those are the prey, trying to pro-create while they can."

She sensed truth and true worry — and his desire to reach her. Her gaze didn't falter. *I believe you* — the slightest mental touch she was able to give, but it sufficed.

"It's off-season. Creatures of the season go into hiding during the day, come out at night to feed. Darkness shields them, the trees shield them, and sometimes, our verandah roof shields them — or so they think. That's when we hear the truth."

Hear? He volunteered the explanation next, while she took another sip.

"It's truly pitch dark outside. The cameras won't catch anything, and the infrared's just a blur. The next morning, before the rain, we see the mess, the tiny scraps of gore spread all over the walkway. That's no sight for the faint-hearted."

So much for option four. Three sounded much more

favorable now — except for the prospect of being locked in this building all night together with the officials and their *muscle*.

"Do you have any idea when the next ship might come here?"

"Nay. The *Hispaniola* does a regular run to Klondike, leaves orders behind for the next ship or messenger drone to pick them up, and there are several merchants for the delivery. There are some other remote locations to be serviced, easier to reach than Klondike, where other shipments come and go. On average, we have five to six merchants per kilocycle — sometimes several within a few days, sometimes not even one for thirty tencycles. Of course, there are some charter liners during the season, but not now."

"How long is the season?"

"Three kilocycles — but it's just over. The next three kilocycles, we're off-season."

"Low traffic."

"Yes."

Syreen wouldn't ask for the room prices in a venue for rich brats. Estoril had been generous, but rent for thirty tencycles and more would overstrain her budget.

The bartender's thoughts ran in the same direction. "You need a room."

"Yes."

"And can't afford it."

"No."

"Too bad."

He pretended to consider her situation, but she sensed his intentions. No, she wouldn't warm his bed. Instead, she emptied her glass. "Thanks for the drink. I'll have a look around."

CHAPTER FOURTEEN

Syreen had absolutely no clue what she was up against, but she didn't feel worried at all when she stepped out on the boardwalk, turned left and walked toward the building corner.

She had fought a hostile flotilla with no more than a corvette, had attacked a dreadnaught with no more than a skirmisher. Impossible odds were her favorite pastime. What harm could some predatory animal do her?

She felt strong, and after the first few steps between the trees, her senses adapted and reached out. Hunger, fear, caution, pain—those were the emotions around her. The human feelings behind her already faded to insignificance. She could hear a freight shuttle taking off, but it somehow didn't matter to her.

More fear and caution to her right, more hunger to her left—she turned left. Only incidentally, she took note of her surroundings—the muddy ground, the tall trees, the light undergrowth, all those dirtside peculiarities that should attract her curiosity . . . but didn't.

She wasn't here as a tourist or researcher. She was here as a predator.

Nor was she curious about how the local creatures would look. If at all, she was curious about how they'd taste. Most importantly, she was excited—no, thrilled—about the hunt.

With the abundance of emotions around her, she could tell major differences apart, but was unable to locate individual sources. As she couldn't read tracks—she couldn't even tell if there were any — she had no clue how to find the seasonal predators except for one option, by putting out a bait.

She was the tasty bit put on display for those who'd come to see. Sleeveless shirt, tight shorts, muddy boots — a lot of exposed skin to taste.

However, the only creatures coming close were swarms of tiny flying things, hovering around her, darting in, almost touching her, then leaving. When she raised a hand to brush some sweat off her face and the creatures dived for some drops, she understood — they were coming to drink.

Perhaps I should be glad not to appeal to them.

Suddenly, a wave of hunger almost overwhelmed her, and then a creature twice as tall as herself shot forward from behind a tree with small eyes, gaping jaw, two rows of finger-long, sharp teeth, long forearms with likewise sharp and even longer claws.

Go straight.

She dodged to the side. Unable to deny her command, the predator kept its direction. When its long neck passed her, she jumped, slung her arms and legs around, and sunk her fangs deep into its thick, leathery skin.

Hunger. Pain. Puzzlement. Heated fluid, a rush of new strength, shallow aftertaste — her victim slowed down to a halt, dropped its body, defenseless.

There came more blood than she could possibly hold, but she didn't have to. She only sucked its power, letting the waste fluid run. The smell of fresh blood filled the air, and she could sense other interested creatures picking up the news. A feast for the scavengers . . . and a signal for other predators.

So she couldn't afford to stay and rest. After a brief glimpse at the creature's body — four times as long as she was tall from fangs to tail, all muscles and bones, no fur, strong hind legs, long front legs with those claws — she decided to leave. The claws would be a powerful weapon if she knew how to handle them, and if she knew how to take them off the creature in the first place.

Syreen felt great. With long strides, she advanced deeper into the forest. Nothing could stop her.

CHAPTER FIFTEEN

Darkness came quick, like a hatch sliding closed. The lack of familiar vision was inconvenient, but it didn't become entirely dark. Syreen found she could still see the contours of trees and branches, so she decided to walk on. After what the bartender had told her, the night was the time to be alert. She had to sleep, but she'd do that in the morning.

When another predator like the first crossed her way, she made short work of it. This time, she gained a broken claw — with its sharp edge and point, it would be a useful tool even outside a fight.

Again, she felt excited and stronger afterward. This was no bad way to live — getting stronger each time — but something was missing. This wasn't the life she wanted to live. She was born for space.

She stopped short. *Am I really feeling happy after that kill? Did I even consider if it's necessary? What happened to me?*

Syreen imagined her inner beast mischievously smiling at her. *Okay, you caught me off-guard, and perhaps it was in a way inevitable, but now we stop that game, yes? Let's try to stay away from conflict, not to alarm the powers that be.*

If that was still possible. At the edge of her empathic perception she felt a new presence growing stronger and slowly approaching. There was hunger, too, but no fear nor caution, only the awareness of unchallenged power.

To relate this to the bartender's story required no mental efforts. Now approached the creature even experienced locals feared enough to not go out at night.

It didn't move fast. At the current speed, she had a cycle or two to make up her mind — should she move in a different direction or have a closer look, or even challenge it?

This time, it wasn't her inner beast daring her, but her own curiosity — or recklessness? It would be interesting to see whether her newfound powers would give her sufficient advantage to defeat that creature.

However, should she fail, her mission would be over. There was too much at stake to take such unnecessary chances — perhaps she should have considered that before she turned the bartender's offer down and left the building's safety?

Such musings weren't helpful now. She decided to stay on the safe side and move out of the creature's way. A little walk would gain her safe distance.

There was a big difference between a forest and open space or even hyperspace, but in one regard, it was all the same — it was easy to recognize an enemy on interception course. The more she went out of its original way, the more that powerful presence changed its direction, too, unerringly coming toward her. Aside from the prospect of having to fight it, one aspect was truly appalling — the creature had to be able to sense her presence.

There was no point in trying to run — where to, after all? Surely the port doors were firmly locked at night. There was no point in hiding, either.

In this regard, again, there was no difference from her previous battles. Spaceships couldn't hide in space, where *Assiduous* surely was an exception. Against a larger enemy, she had to rely on speed, swiftness, precision, and her fighting skills.

Fighting skills, hah! She had enjoyed the same martial arts instructions as all Duchy officer candidates, but later, as skirmisher pilot, she hadn't had much opportunity to practice them. She had some practice in biting victims . . . which were already stunned or distracted by her mental powers. From its mental presence, she knew the new hunter had to be resistant if not immune to her mental powers. Certainly she had no practice at all in fighting such a large, strong animal with bare hands—and fangs.

SitOps—I'm in the middle of an alien forest, surrounded by countless alien predators, one of which can sense my location and is coming for me. Options—running, won't work. Hiding, won't work. Fighting—impossible odds.

If you can't win, change the rules. Lateral thinking, my instructors told me—and next, they made very clear what would happen to anyone not sticking to the Books. Which I did anyway.

That's why I'm still alive. However, how can I act against the Books if there are no instructions for this planet?

She looked up and tried to see the stars, space, her true home.

I should be up there . . .

CHAPTER SIXTEEN

Space pilots shouldn't suffer from vertigo, one of Syreen's instructors had said. A skirmisher in stealth mode, sailing space without drive, in free fall, is scary enough without such a condition.

So she shouldn't fear heights . . . if only her imagination would agree with her and stop conjuring pictures of her smashed body on the forest floor.

If humans were meant to climb . . . hadn't her biology teacher mentioned something of primates, distant relatives, ancient creatures living in trees? She had to credit him with something. After sacrificing her boots, she had indeed managed to climb a tree, at least most of it, to the first larger branches. Now, looking down, she understood how tall these trees truly were.

Which was a good thing. If her first two victims were in any way exemplary for the wildlife on this planet, and her menace was in any way like them, it wasn't built for climbing at all. That should give her an advantage in the fight.

Now that she was up in the tree, she had to wait. At least she was used to patient waiting.

The creature announced its coming with the crushing of larger undergrowth branches. Syreen braced herself for the fight to come. Although smart actions were surely not to be neglected, this wouldn't primarily be a battle of minds, but a dirty, gory, painful, hands-on fight for survival.

She pulled the claw from her shorts waistband and

checked how to hold it best, so that she could use it without cutting her own finger off. However, to be useful in battle, she needed a firm grip and a way to apply force.

If I hold it by the rounded upper edge . . .

With a sigh, she drove the tip into the tree bark. Applying the unfamiliar tool would require too much of her attention. She had to do without.

When it passes below me, puzzled not to find anything, I jump down and bite . . .

There were multiple flaws in her strategy, which she found out when the creature approached between the next trees.

First, she wouldn't see when and where to jump. The animal was almost invisible in the dark, even to her enhanced senses. All she could recognize was the place where it obstructed other contours she could otherwise see.

Second, that obstructing shape was huge—the creature was at least twice as large as the other predators, so if its skin was also twice as thick, she would have a hard time piercing it with her fangs.

Third, it wouldn't pass below her. The dark shape closed the remaining distance slowly, and the mental presence—in its head?—rose almost to the level of her branches. There was no jumping down on it—and it knew precisely where to look for her, with no moment of surprise.

In any case, it didn't attack. There was no hunger or rage, only curiosity and—amusement?

Without visual perception—or had it?—they faced each other in motionless anticipation.

CHAPTER SEVENTEEN

Syreen hadn't yet made her mind up whether the situation should be scary or funny. In any case, the being before her radiated neither hostility nor malice, and she didn't feel compelled to fight either.

Peace, she thought.

Her opponent's amusement grew, but there was another emotion, too—pride. It felt like a claim. The creature claimed respect.

She was quite aware of their difference in size, but size didn't matter, as she had proven several times.

Respect you can have, but not surrender. This is your turf, you're the ruler here. But I didn't come to bow before you. I can claim respect, too.

What did her mental statement translate into? It shouldn't come across as defiance, as offensive, but she wouldn't want to appear intimidated, either.

I demand to be tolerated.

She wasn't prepared for the sudden blow of air that sent her off-balance. She managed to get hold of the claw—but pulled it out of the tree, and then she fell. She twisted around in mid-air and came down on her feet and one hand—no time to wonder how she had survived that deep drop unharmed—ready to fight, when something hard hit her chest—*ouch*—and sent her flying again.

This time, she landed on her back—*ouch*—tensed her muscles to jump up again, when something painfully sharp grazed her chest in three places, from one shoulder to her breast, from below the other breast to her side, and from her side to her hipbone.

Ouch!

Three parallel cuts, not deep enough to cut her ribs, but still dangerous with regard to the loss of blood, and terribly painful. If she moved, she'd tear her own tissue further apart, thus sealing her fate. But wasn't her fate already sealed? Another such strike would cut her in half, and there was nothing she could do about it. *Too much pain.*

The strike didn't come. Her opponent's amusement was gone, the curiosity faded, the claim for respect remained, and now, she sensed a reserved acceptance.

Point taken. I'm tolerated, but not welcome.

And I won't die tonight.

Instead, she remained motionless and focused on her wounds. There was an unfamiliar, itching, tingling warmth. Syreen could feel her cuts grow back together. She could also feel the healing effort consuming a large share of her power, but within a few centicycles, her cuts had closed, the pain faded.

She pushed herself up until her hand touched the claw she had lost upon dropping, then struggled back to her feet.

Her opponent made another move toward her. His emotions radiated a warning. She wouldn't get past him even to collect her boots.

Okay, okay. I will leave.

CHAPTER EIGHTEEN

Without her boots, Syreen's walk back to the spaceport was a torture. Pointy broken branches, pieces of bark, wooden chips, scratchy roots and whatever there might be made every step an adventure. Soon she lost count of the splinters in her feet.

There could have been much to contemplate, but she stopped thinking about anything but the immediate *Here and Now*. Another step across this branch, and the second foot, and another over that root, and to this tree and around . . .

Morning came, and with it the light, and a moment after she had reached the boardwalk, the promised rain started pouring down.

When the bartender opened the steel door to the board-walk and spotted her, a loud "Gal!" escaped him. Next, she stumbled and fell into his strong arms, which lifted her and carried her inside.

He gently let her down on a table. "Gal, what did you do? Outside all night!"

Another voice chimed in. "Who's that? What happened to her?"

She recognized the voice as that of the port authority officer who had waved her through.

"The star angel who arrived with *Hispaniola*. Uh—Syreen was her name. She went outside yesterday and I didn't see her return. Thought she might be with you or your boys."

Syreen tried to support herself on one arm. Firm hands held her down. "No, lie down and relax. You're hurt."

The other man spoke up again. "Are those cuts?"

The bartender reached for the claw in her hand. "What's this? Look, Joe, a sauroid foreclaw."

"She must have found it somewhere," Joe said.

"Looks rather like she fought for it," the bartender objected.

"Who fought for what?" a third voice sounded from the inner door. Steps approached her table, and then she looked up into the face of a bearded man.

"Syreen," she introduced herself. *Is that weak voice mine?*

"I'm Barney, head of the local guard. You got some wounds there indeed — cut through the shirt, I reckon? You were lucky they didn't go deeper. Those sauroids deal out powerful strikes. Sorry, but your rags must go. They can't hide your pretty chest anyway." There was a ripping noise, and then he held some rust-red fabric up over her face. "Soaked with blood all over. If all that came from your cuts, I wonder why they're not bleeding now."

"Not all my blood," she whispered. "I killed two sauroids."

"Two? How?"

"With my bare hands, how else?" she tried to joke.

"Impossible," Joe said. "You need a blaster or a railgun to kill a sauroid."

Barney placed a thumb on the scar at her hipbone and spread his fingers until he could reach the next cut. "This was no sauroid."

"No," she agreed.

"But, Barney . . ." the bartender said.

"No, Rico," Barney answered. "The claws are too far apart for a sauroid. We know of only one creature that does such wide strikes."

CHAPTER NINETEEN

Syreen felt weak. All the strength she had gained on her way out had been consumed on her walk back—healing the severe wounds, keeping them closed, keeping her up and walking, and mending the worst injuries on her feet. She had nothing left to give, couldn't even reach out to sense the men's emotions.

Rico brought her a cup of hot forwine, and Barney helped her to sit up on the table. The movement caused pain in her belly—the wounds were closed, but still hurt.

"You met one," Barney said.

Syreen nodded, keeping the warm cup between her hands and smelling the intense forwine aroma.

"It hurt you, but it didn't kill you. Why?"

"Maybe I don't smell right, don't taste right. But primarily I assume *he* didn't want to. This strike—" she looked down her front with the three bright-red lines across the rust-brown skin—"must've been meant as a warning. I'm not welcome out there."

"A stupid animal?" Joe objected. "It's a killer!"

Barney glanced over his shoulder. "Hush, Joe. The facts before our own eyes can't be denied. She *is* alive."

"And tells stories."

The local head of guard faced her again and rolled his eyes. She had to suppress a giggle and quickly raised the cup to her lips.

"She could have caused the wounds herself, with that claw," Joe went on.

Barney took the claw and held it up. "Only, there's no blood on this claw. Syreen, what will we find when we analyze the blood on your shirt?"

"A lot of my own, plus that of the two sauroids I killed." She focused on him. "And whatever *he* had on his claws."

"What did he look like?" Rico asked.

Syreen shrugged. "Black. A big blot of black, before a black background. Sorry, I didn't really see him."

"How can you tell his gender then?" Barney asked.

She shrugged again. "He felt male—I don't know. Female intuition. Or the way he smelled." Only now she realized that there had been a distinct smell, too—during her encounter completely masked by his mental presence. "A kind of musk. Perhaps sperm. I can't really define it."

Barney nodded. "We might find out. With the victims those creatures leave at our doorstep every few nights, we occasionally find traces of their DNA, probably from their saliva. We can compare that with the stuff you brought."

"She's still telling us lies," Joe insisted. "Kill a sauroid. How?"

Barney focused on her. "Yes, how? I'm curious, too."

"I tricked one into running head-first into a tree," she said. "It didn't do it any good. No big deal to stab its throat."

"And why?"

"So that it couldn't kill me first, of course. Oh—and I needed something to drink."

"Drink?"

She lifted her cup. "Blood. Awful taste, but it keeps you alive. However, I'd always prefer this forwine. Good stuff."

CHAPTER TWENTY

With the second cup of forwine, at least a little life returned into Syreen, and with it returned her clairsentience. Barney and Rico radiated true concern, perhaps some protective instinct, while Joe still nurtured disbelief and aversion, although mixed with some sexual tension. Unlike the two others, he wasn't oblivious to her partial nudity.

Barney had started to tend to her feet. "This is no place to go outside barefoot."

"No. I had to leave my boots behind when I ran away from him."

"Why did you take them off in the first place? Hurting feet?"

"No. I couldn't climb in them."

"Climb?"

"I thought I could hide up in a tree. Didn't work—he spotted me there."

Barney paused, one welcome warm hand around her right ankle. "And then?"

"He exhaled and blew me off my branch."

"You fell?"

"I managed to drop onto my feet and arms—learned that during free fall training, some winters ago. Next, he gave me that friendly pat." She placed the almost-empty cup down and followed one fresh scar with her right index finger. "Hurt like hell, but luckily he didn't cut deep. Plus I'm healing fast."

"Indeed. You're more than lucky."

"Perhaps because she's a star angel," Rico chimed in.

"Star angel?" Barney asked. "What's that?"

"It's a term coined by the merchant guild for people bringing luck to the ship they're traveling with. Some say it's superstition — it's difficult to tell, because it rarely happens."

"Well." Barney briefly gazed at her face, then continued his work at her foot. "Captain Estoril was lucky. He didn't buy the usual stuff for his makeshift repairs. His ship came out of this run better than ever before. Hardly any wear, so that he could afford parts for long-term maintenance. Call it coincidence he brought a star angel, but it's remarkable."

"I didn't know that," Rico said. "That *is* remarkable."

After a last gentle rub, Barney placed her foot down and took the other. "Okay?"

"Very good," she said with a purr in her voice. "It's almost worth the pain I had to literally walk through."

The head of guard sighed. There was no greed, no malice in him.

"You know what, Syreen? You remind me of my daughter." He plucked a splinter out of her sole. "She was a nice girl. Always confident, always happy. And so pretty — all the boys were after her. Like her mother, of course."

There was sadness in his voice.

She sensed Joe about to chime in, and silenced him. *Find something to do.* It took her a little effort and consumed a larger share of her remaining power than she had expected, but she felt it was worth it.

"What happened to her?"

"*I* happened to her." His grip around her foot tightened, and she suppressed a wheeze. "It would be easy to blame it on her mother. We had grown apart in a way. Stayed together out of habit — and for our daughter, of course. At first, I didn't notice the change. Disagreements turned to quarrels. Frustration grew — it affected my job, and the stress there affected our relationship. A downward spiral. Then my wife started to cheat on me—and tease me with it. She dressed up in sexy clothes and went out to meet other men, gave them what she denied to me. I should have found a way to vent my frustration, but I refused to consider paying her back in the same coin. I could have taken a whore—that might have been better. Instead, I helped myself, at home, when she was away, when I thought I was alone."

He gazed down at her foot. "Our daughter came home early. She caught me in action. I . . . I didn't find the words to explain. Worse, that day, as young adult girls did then, she was wearing just body paint and a tiny thong. She tried to be understanding, came closer to comfort me, and then, it just happened, and I was inside her. I should've stopped, but I couldn't."

Very gently, he removed another splinter. "Her mother learned about it, and that was it. I had to leave. I couldn't look her in the eye anymore, couldn't bear the thought of being on the same planet with her. As far away as possible I had to go—and now I'm here."

She leaned forward until she could touch his shoulder. "You regret it."

"Every day of my life."

His sincere regret was so clear to her. She glanced around. Joe had left. Rico was still listening, radiating concern, but also compassion.

"Did you tell her?"

"No."

"You have to."

"I . . . I can't. When I think of her, I see her naked, colored body, and I . . ."

She squeezed his shoulder. "You need help."

Barney looked up. "Help?"

"You need me."

"But . . ."

"As I am now. Nothing but body paint. A different picture on your mind."

Rico pulled a token from his pocket. "You need a room."

The guard took it and looked at her foot. "Uh . . ."

"Carry me."

CHAPTER TWENTY-ONE

Her victim was unable to resist — guilt, shame, frustration, loneliness, regret, love, passion, lust, protective instinct, and then the sight of her blood-covered boobs, all together formed a recipe that worked even better than her mental powers.

When he placed her down on the neat and clean hotel bed, she sensed a last hint of doubt in him.

"Lift my legs," she asked.

Confused, he did as ordered. Only resting on her shoulders, she could now easily push her shorts over her buttocks.

"Let me down."

She pulled her knees close, shoved the shorts over them, flicked the shorts away with her treated foot, and then slowly placed her legs down.

"Uh, wait, I . . ."

"Come." She reached out a hand, grabbed his, and pulled him closer until he had to lean over her. Her lips searched his for a passionate kiss. Next, he lost his balance and stumbled down on her.

Syreen wrapped her arms and legs around him. Her hug gave him time to familiarize with his situation — resting on a naked female's chest and between her wide-spread thighs.

When he paused their kiss to regain his breath, she collected a little of her remaining strength and rolled them around. Now he was reclining on his back under her. She moved her knees up and close, so that she could sit up over his lap.

His gaze wouldn't stick to her bare breasts, but followed the bright pink scars, returned to her tits, then down the streaks again, and along her crotch — the sauroids' blood hadn't stopped at her waistline, but soaked her shorts, too, and anything underneath. Her *body paint* was everywhere.

"You're lucky to be alive still," he said.

"Hush." She placed one finger on his lips, took his hand with her other, and moved it around her boob. "Make me feel alive."

Leaning forward, she moved his other hand up, too. His fingers began to explore her curves, felt around her areolas, and then caressed her firmly erect nipples. His eyes filled with tears.

Her smile, her wide-open eyes, her joyous sighs should encourage him further. Again she leaned down to kiss him, and when he took his hands off her chest to hug her and pull her tight, she didn't object.

However, hugging alone wouldn't do — neither for her nor for him. With her pelvis, she began slow moves against his lap, and soon felt something growing against her pubes.

Now one of his hands explored her buttocks, while the other checked for her tit again. His kiss became hungrier, more demanding, and she answered in kind. With one hand, she reached down, between them, began to caress the outside of his pants. He wheezed.

He didn't protest when she sat up, leaned back, and searched for his fly. A moment later, his erect member rose before her, trembling with anticipation. He was so tense, she feared he would come the very moment she touched his glans — so she grabbed his cock at the base, adjusted its aim, and quickly wrapped her own vagina around it.

She found out she wasn't ready. "Ouch!"

As expected, he moaned and came. A moment later, he made a sad face. "Sorry."

Syreen smiled and caressed his cheek. "Don't worry. This was just the beginning."

"I hurt you."

"I wasn't as ready as I thought. Don't worry. Next time, I'll be wet for you."

"Next time?"

She leaned down and kissed him. "You don't think I'll let you get away that easily, do you?"

Chapter Twenty-two

Syreen touched his limp member with a finger, but it didn't stir. Had that single shot depleted him?

Perhaps there was another way. She turned around and placed her legs on both sides of his shoulders. She felt the pull at her labia — despite the sticky goo, she felt herself gaping. Still, this sight wasn't enough to turn him on.

So she leaned down, adjusted his limp tool with one hand, and placed her lips around its tip. That enticed an "Oh," and she felt a little reply in her hand.

The success let her continue the task. Of course, she had practiced oral intercourse before, and she knew that, despite its common term, it wasn't about pumping her breath into it, but it still felt unfamiliar to her — no, she didn't like it at all.

She probed with her tongue. *Yuck. Let's not think about taste.* Now she felt his cock growing into her mouth. His defenselessness turned her on. *You can't resist me, not if I really take to the task, even without mind control.*

A few more licks, and he was hard as a rock.

Full of his — blood. Close.

She felt her canines grow.

No. Not this way.

Syreen let him go, rose, and quickly changed her riding position again. She probed her own readiness, found herself sufficiently aroused and wet, and slid down his shaft. Her victim moaned again, but this time he didn't come right away.

So she slowly started moving her pelvis, and when he started to answer her with his own pushes, she leaned down to his throat. *Now, in exchange for a passionate encounter you'll never forget, you will contribute to my recovery.*

CHAPTER TWENTY-THREE

Syreen woke up when her host stirred. Snuggled into his left arm, her head on his shoulder, she felt comfortably protected. That was a weird thought, as the only threat around was she herself.

"Oooh, what a dream," Barney moaned. Then his left hand twitched, twitched a second time, and his right hand came across and touched her shoulder.

She pushed herself up and moved closer to his face. "Good morning, Barney." She placed a gentle kiss on his lips, gave him a moment to notice, and then she started pulling at his lips for another passionate French kiss.

Her left hand slowly wandered down, where his cock was still sticking out of his open fly. When she touched it, he wheezed, and when it quickly grew into her hand, she started stroking it rhythmically.

"Ooohnoooyyyeeesss . . ."

Syreen knew she wasn't ready again yet. Luckily, her host was willing to change that—he started caressing her tit, her shoulder, the part of her buttocks he could reach, and when she allowed him to move his left arm, he intensified his efforts.

Soon she was on her back and he was knocking at her door—that is, he was beating her clitoris with the tip of his cock.

Next, he leaned down and kissed her again. While their lips and tongues were engaged, the movements of his pelvis slowly rubbed his boner along her pubes. Very successfully, she had triggered his passion, but hadn't triggered her own. He was about to fix that, and she enjoyed his efforts. Where had he learned those skills?

Syreen felt his desire, and she really appreciated how he held back, focused on her needs alone. In fact, he was too reluctant.

"Fuck me. I need you inside me. Now. Hard. Deep."

She braced herself for his first thrust. He did as asked—a probe, brief pause to aim, a firm move with his hip, and he penetrated her, all the way in. Yes, she was ready, and yet the sudden push hurt—it was a welcome kind of pain, as she needed to feel his power, his life.

His passion *required* another bite—not to suck more of his blood, although her beast would take all it could, but to share their sensations. *Can I control it?*

I will control it.

She did, and she shared her passionate lust with him, as he shared his passion with her. Together they reached another extraordinarily satisfying climax. But there was more, and that complicated things. He had fallen in love with her.

CHAPTER TWENTY-FOUR

He stood before their bed and gazed down on her, or through her. He radiated worries, but Syreen resisted the temptation to dig deeper in his emotions.

"You need a shower," he said.

"You must take your samples first," she objected. "Otherwise I have to go out tonight and get some more."

Barney made a face, but quickly fetched a small device from his pockets, leaned forward and placed it on her bloodstained skin in several places. It beeped each time. Finally, he tucked it away and stepped back. For a while, he remained silent.

"You need to return to work?" she asked.

"Aw, no. They won't miss me soon. Rico saw us heading off to his room, so they all know what's going on. As long as nobody causes trouble—and the *Hispaniola* people surely won't—I can take as much time off as I need." There was regret in his voice. "We don't have many female visitors, and if we do, usually they're ship's cats, you know? Fair game for everyone around, until they leave with their crew. That's standard procedure."

"So you followed standard procedure."

"Until now, I didn't, I left the girls to the others. But this time—well, you know."

"I know. That's why I did it—you needed to work on that memory."

"I'm grateful. You were very kind—no, you were a force of nature, irresistible. But once we leave this room, the others

63

will demand their share of you."

She shrugged. "I'm not surprised. That's why I went outside last night, you know? To get away from their demands. And because I can't afford a room."

"No? But . . . you're no ship's cat."

"No. I know what you think. Interstellar travelers should be rich. I'm not. I couldn't afford the passage."

"But how . . ."

"I'm a star angel, entitled to travel for free on any merchant ship. It's up to them to invite me for free meals, but they're supposed to take me along. That's how I came here." She sat up. "I know that status won't buy me anything here. Tell me—does that *fair game* rule apply to independent women, too?"

"Not if they arrive with their own team. But you're alone, even more once *Hispaniola* leaves. That's why I'm worried."

Syreen pushed herself forward to the edge of the bed and rose—with caution. But her feet didn't hurt anymore. "So I'm alone against a whole bunch of guys, each of whom wants to get into my pants. They think they're entitled to it, they have the legal power to demand it, and they have the real power to enforce it, right?"

"That's about it, yes."

"Worse, I have no shirt and no shoes anymore. However, I'm the one who killed two sauroids with my bare hands. Consider that."

She left to go to the hygiene unit. On her way, she picked up her shorts, the only item she owned now, and the only item worth a refresher treatment—aside from Estoril's credit chip.

CHAPTER TWENTY-FIVE

When Syreen returned to Rico's shop, it was late afternoon again. Her stomach loudly reminded her of having been neglected for so long.

Joe was sitting at a table with two of the guards. He looked up and smiled at her. "Barney didn't feed you enough, gal. Would you like to taste my juice?"

She did not smile when she focused on him. "Later, perhaps."

The two guards stared at her with wide eyes. She couldn't blame them for taking advantage of her daring appearance, but she quickly turned her back on them and ambled down one aisle.

She tried a pair of self-adapting boots, added a checkered shirt, and wondered whether she could afford them. Imported goods were always expensive, everywhere, and there was no local produce on Appalahoo. When she walked up to the counter, the guards' stares were again fixed on her bare boobs.

"How much?" she asked Rico.

The price he asked was ridiculous even for a planet this remote. "I'm not buying a new hyperdrive, Rico."

He shrugged. "Take it or leave it."

"How much is a meal and a beer?"

She sensed a pang of guilt in him when he quoted another outrageous amount and gazed past her. In Joe's direction, she noticed.

A pity. Rico had been quite nice in the morning. Now he

was just another asshole. So he was *fair game* for her, too.

You'll be first. But I won't have sex with any of you. I'll take your strength, that's all I need.

Syreen had just finished the last of her four victims, ordered him to forget, and watched the skin over the bite mark close, when another score of guards entered Rico's shop and cheered at the sight of her.

She bent backward and presented her tits to the spectators. "Who's first?"

One of them stepped forward, smiling and rocking his pelvis. She grabbed his hand, placed it on her chest, and smiled at the others. "Why don't you let your pants down and jerk off?"

Her subsequent mental command gave them no choice but to obey. While she drank from her latest victim, the other guards started stroking their cocks. In the order they finished, she let them parade past her, offer their necks to her bite, and then march off.

To the last, she said, "Go get the others."

She didn't pause until she had consumed a large blood donation from each of them, with the exception of Barney, who was still busy with her samples in the laboratory. Only then did she loosen her mental grip. *You had a hot evening, and now you're totally worn out.*

Next, she turned to Rico. "What was the price for dinner, again?" *True rates.*

For a still expensive, but more reasonable price, she enjoyed her meal with a beer and purchased boots and shirt.

"Make sure you close the doors behind me. I feel like another evening stroll outside."

CHAPTER TWENTY-SIX

Syreen felt like bursting with power. What a difference! Not one, not two donators—two dozen of them, strong men, each an abundant source of life. Each of them eager to spend his semen for her—wasted to the floor, with two well-hung exceptions. It would have been a shame not to ride their extraordinarily large cocks. They had simply looked too tasty.

They had been tasty. Indeed, their blood was more spicy when she rode them, perhaps due to the emotions it carried?

In any case, all their contributions had made her stronger than ever. She felt almost ready to face her big opponent again. *This time, you won't cut my skin, Biggie.*

Was it madness? Returning to the forest, despite his warning? She wouldn't get away with a graze again. Either she won, or she died. But she felt too strong to die. Not this night, not here, not by this *animal*.

I must prove to myself that I can stand my ground. Otherwise, there's no point in continuing my mission into the very heart of the enemy.

She followed a different direction this time. She wasn't eager to meet the rotten corpses of her two previous victims again, nor the scavengers that might have joined the feast. Moreover, she needed some distance from her nemesis' mental presence until she had completed her preparations.

Ahead, she sensed at least three of the smaller sauroids.

Smaller, but still more than twice my size. In this case, however, size doesn't matter.

Like the night before, the big bad boy eventually sensed her presence in *his* forest again. He wasn't amused, he wasn't curious, and he wasn't cautious. He came for her at full speed, and he was really fast.

Syreen eyed a strong branch above her head, farther up above ground. She wouldn't be safer there, any more than the night before.

Calm. I've picked my place with care. Everything will be fine.

She wiggled her bare toes. Although she fully trusted her skills and her plan, she had left her boots in a safe place, together with her shirt and shorts. She could pick them up on her way back.

There will be blood. There will be prey. I'm the bait.

The clear air carried the sound of crushing wood. Some trees were collateral damage tonight. There wasn't much else — a gentle breeze, her own breath's sound, her heartbeat, a predator's tang, barely restrained hunger, but most of all the beast's rage.

Her own rage, growing inside her, ready to lash out.

Calm. Not yet.

He came bursting through the trees, covering two or three times his own length in each leap, the forest floor trembling under each step's impact. His ire drowned out any other emotion.

Syreen braced herself. *Prepare.*

The monster had to slow down — she had picked two strong trees growing relatively close to each other, too strong for him to smash through them, and too close to easily jump around them.

Now.

Oblivious to his surroundings, the absolute, unchallenged ruler, focused on his single, insolent target, he was vulnerable to the coordinated attack of six sauroids coming for his legs, his throat, and his neck.

Legs — don't let go. Throat — hold on. Neck — retreat. Mount — stay.

Howling in pain and rage, the large monster ran against a tree — would have smashed the neck biter, if the sauroid hadn't followed her mental command.

The scene was difficult to control in the utter darkness, but she could see, hear, and smell not just with her own enhanced senses, but also with those of her team — seven sauroids she had sought out, brought under her mental control, and bitten to establish a deeper link. Forced to be hunting alone for the smaller prey, alone too weak and too small to challenge the much larger creature, sauroids couldn't win such a battle in this forest — unless a mastermind concerted them.

All to the right leg. Bring him down.

Again, the ground trembled when the mighty monster dropped on its side.

Mount — throat. Get hold.

Her mount — the seventh sauroid — leaned down and struck with its claws, and then with its jaws.

Great. Hold tight.

She climbed forward, glided down her mount's neck, stepped on its nose, and jumped onto the monster's body — quickly grabbed hold at a deep wound in its neck, torn by a first bite, leaned down, and sank her own fangs into the tough flesh.

The intense rage, now mixed with never-before-experienced fear, almost overwhelmed her. She fought for her mental balance, but only a moment, and then she was in control again.

You are mine. I'm the master. You deny me respect, you pay the price.

CHAPTER TWENTY-SEVEN

The first rays of daylight fell on the boardwalk before the spaceport, followed by early raindrops. Barney nodded at Rico and pointed his rifle at the door.

"Can't we wait until after the rain?" one guard asked.

Barney gave him a stern glance. "She might be injured. One cycle late might be too late. We're going now."

Neither of the other five men of his little team objected. Barney knew that they weren't eager to venture into the deep forest, but they were supposed to follow his command and didn't dare to oppose him. At least they didn't while he watched them.

Rico opened the lock and pushed the door open. One guard gasped, another wheezed, and a third pressed his rifle against his chest.

"By all ghosts in space," Rico whispered.

Barney turned around, not sure what to expect except the usual gray curtain of morning rain.

The rain was there, of course, but it couldn't veil the silhouettes of seven sauroids, lined up like a well-trained guard unit on the spacefield. Trained reflexes took command, and he started to raise his rifle. But they didn't move, so he paused.

The one on the center was somewhat deformed, however . . . no. He squinted. It carried something in its mouth—a sauroid head? Only three times as large—and what was that bump on its back? A bump that now waved at him . . . a rider.

He walked out into the rain.

"Eh—boss?" one of his men said.

"Wait there."

One of the sauroids shook his head, and he clenched his rifle. When the creature didn't move further, he made a few more steps.

"Close enough," a familiar female voice said. "They're still a bit nervous."

"Syreen? What are you doing there?"

"Collecting evidence."

"What do you mean?"

"First, if you analyze this head, you'll find traces of the same DNA as the one at my cuts. I want to be sure I got that bastard. Second, this is a demonstration."

"A demonstration?"

"Yes, and you should go and get Joe out here. He should see with his own eyes who's got the real power here—and what happens to creatures who cross me."

He heard her words, and he saw her sitting on the sauroid's back, but his brain still refused to accept the fact. Images of past hunting accidents came to his mind, stories of other almost fatal encounters with such creatures, their own safety instructions—never go into the forest alone, wear rifle, helmet, armor, never stay outside an armored shelter at night, and avoid the forest altogether off-season—plus the gory fragments of such sauroids at their doorsteps, left behind by a fierce monster that no man had seen before.

Here before his own eyes he had the proof, the wet black skin, the huge eyes, terrifying, underarm-long fangs of a monster created to kill, one of the most dangerous predators known to mankind—or better, so far unknown to mankind— defeated by a single, unarmed woman.

Her mount dropped the beast's head and snorted.

No, not unarmed. He looked up and smiled. "I'll go and get Joe, if he's not already on his way. I agree—he must see this."

71

Chapter Twenty-eight

Syreen felt a rising pressure between her butt cheeks from Barney's morning wood. Soon he'd wake up, feel her buttocks at his cock and her left breast under his right hand and realize his wet dreams were still true. She wanted to be ready for him, so she began to move her pelvis and reached between her legs to feel herself up. From the evening before, her labia was still sticky.

Her thighs were sticky, too, but that didn't matter.

She opened her mind for the other men's emotions. Barney wasn't the only guard with wet dreams and a boner in the morning, but he was the one with exclusive access to her pussy—because she wanted it that way. That way, she had a comfy bed, a comfy lover, and didn't stir fantasies about a lonely lady in a lonely room.

There were other fantasies galore. The entire spaceport was wrapped in an invisible aura of lust, and granting those emotions unrestricted access could make a girl get off in an instant. It was a special kind of voyeurism, only mentally watching other men become horny, masturbate, and come to climax, but she didn't feel guilty.

She learned about the new developments before Barney did—someone was torn from his daydream, had to focus on work instead of his cock, and a moment later, Barney's com chimed.

Barney woke up, took his hand off her tit, rolled away from her and waved at the com. "Yeah?"

"Ship in orbit. Shuttle expected in a quartercycle. Prepare

for visitors."

"Yeah, will do." He waved again. "Yaroslav, have your team ready in twenty. Shuttle landing. I'll be there."

With the third wave, he silenced his com. Next, he rolled back to her. "Maybe a chance for you to leave."

"Yes. Interested in a last quickie?"

"Does it rain in the morning?"

It always rained in the morning. The adverse weather didn't affect shuttle operation, but soaked the space field's already muddy surface and changed it into a slippery adventure. The shuttle crew had a hard time maintaining their footing and arrived at the boardwalk soaking wet, muddy, and with a mouthful of curses.

Syreen watched the spectacle from Rico's door, leaning on the doorframe. Two younger newcomers eyed her curiously, but the entire crew had to visit Joe's port authority office first.

About ten centicycles later, three crew members hurried back to their shuttle through the mud, while the two oldest-looking men entered Rico's venue through the inner door. One had a narrow mustache and the cap and stripes of a merchant captain, the other was bald and clean shaven and wore a work uniform.

They both headed to a table, dropped into chairs, and waved at her.

She ambled up to them. "Hi guys. I'm Syreen. You're new to Appalahoo?"

"Two hot forwine," the captain said.

"I'll tell Rico." She walked over and leaned to the counter. "The Very Important People demand two hot forwine. I felt compelled to relay the message but won't interfere with your business. However, I take a cup for myself."

"Three, then."

"I'll pay one."

"Yes, yes, got it."

"I just wanted to make that clear."

"Sure. No need to call your muscle in."

Syreen gave Rico her nicest predator smile, and he shuddered. Since her little show act, nobody dared to challenge her. Mental control was no longer necessary.

The large monster's head would receive an honorable place above Rico's counter once Barney had prepared it, at the latest before the season started, so that every wannabe hunter knew what he'd be up against.

The holo of her parade already had its place on the counter, where every patron picking up his drink could see it.

Rico placed three steaming cups on the counter. "Here you go."

"Thanks." She held out her credit chip, waited for the old-fashioned flash, and then picked up her cup. When she returned to the table with just one cup, the two guests made puzzled faces.

"Self-service," she said. "May I join you?"

"I thought you were working here," the captain said. "Please accept my apologies. Your name was — Syreen?"

"Yes."

"Let me introduce us. My chief engineer, Horus Johnson. My name is Ubukata. I'm the skipper of the *Narihira*."

"Mr. Johnson, Captain Ubukata, I'm pleased to meet you."

The engineer nodded and left toward the counter.

The captain went on, "May I be so bold — if you're not working here, what are you doing here off-season? Research?"

She smiled. "I had a few encounters with the local wildlife, but I wouldn't call it research. No, I'm waiting for a chance to travel onward."

"Passenger liners, even charter, don't come here off-season."

"I know. I came here from Klondike aboard *Hispaniola*. Her skipper was so kind as to take me along."

Now he eyed her with a different kind of interest. "For only one trip?"

"Which isn't uncommon for passengers. On Klondike, no sane merchant would hire crew, not even a ship's cat. No sane merchant would allow a stranger aboard as passenger either. That's what you wanted to say, wasn't it?"

"But he took you along. I'm trying to imagine the circumstances that could lead to such an unlikely development. Someone must have been very convincing."

"Indeed." She saw the engineer return with the two cups and a very excited expression on his face. "Convincing was my entry in the guild roll as star angel."

CHAPTER TWENTY-NINE

Syreen didn't evade Captain Ubukata's glare. "Our host keeps the guild rolls on Appalahoo. You can ask him, if you don't believe me."

The engineer placed the two cups down on the table. "Is that you in the image on the counter?"

"Yes."

"And those creatures? Tamed mounts? From the stories I heard about Appalahoo, I didn't expect those. They said it's a wild planet."

"It is. Those creatures are predators, and they feed on reckless hunters as easily as on local prey. Go out at night, and you're prey, too."

"But you . . ."

"But I know how to deal with them. After I killed the first two." Syreen knew, once they asked around, they'd hear her story anyway. So she could as well tell them the facts herself. "I needed some aid for hunting down the big one."

"What kind of gun did you use?" Johnson asked.

"I don't have a gun." She spread her arms. "I travel light. What you see is all I own."

"No gun?" He visibly struggled to match her statement with the image of her and the sauroids.

"No gun. That's why I needed the sauroids. Their fangs killed the big one. However, it wasn't easy to make them cooperate, as you can imagine."

The engineer shook his head. "Skipper, you really should have a look for yourself." While he was saying that, Rico approached the table with a pad.

The innkeeper sat down at their table. "I saw your interest in the pic." He let his pad project it over the table. "You might ask whether that's been faked. It wasn't—I saw it myself, right before my door."

Captain and engineer eyed the open door.

"Don't worry. They don't come here in daylight—unless our young lady here summons them. Which she did, and I have no clue how. Fierce, wild creatures you don't want to meet even with a gun in your hand, believe me."

He moved the image to one side—the captain's gaze following it, unable to detach.

"I know Syreen wants to travel on, most likely with you, as there's no other ship in orbit currently. So you want to check whether she really is registered as star angel. I brought the rolls, and I can assure you, she is."

"How's that possible?" the captain asked.

"You must ask her. I have no clue."

Syreen pushed the image farther aside again and leaned forward to gain the captain's attention. "I had the opportunity to help out Captain Kasai."

"Kasai—Noriaki Kasai? Of the *Light of Mandalay?*"

"Yes, the same."

The captain rose. "I met him a long time ago. He's a good captain, and if he felt like nominating a star angel, that must apply to a person he truly trusts—with his life and his ship. His recommendation should suffice for me to take you along, so welcome to the *Narihira.*" With a wave of his hand, he motioned his engineer to hold back. "You know, that is the kind of story that travels a lot faster than light. A merchant boarded by pirates, a warship coming to aid, blackmailed by the pirates—and then, an impossible shot across almost one light minute, tearing the pirate to pieces. That's the stuff legends are made of." He scrutinized her. "Or star angels."

"Fifty light seconds," she said. "My warship was a corvette."

"A *corvette?*"

Syreen shrugged. "It was pure luck I came along. I had to work with what I had."

"This is even more outstanding." Ubukata raised his cup. "I'm honored to meet you. To your health."

Engineer Johnson rose with his own cup. "To your health."

Rico only stared at her. "You commanded a warship?"

"She did," the captain advised him. "And from what I've heard, you wouldn't want to cross her."

"Oh, from what I've seen, I won't, either."

Both glanced at the still visible display.

"Point taken. Salute."

CHAPTER THIRTY

"Ow."

Syreen slowly moved her arms and legs, stretched them, bent them, and then felt for her aching neck. "Ow."

She struggled with her stomach, won, took a deep breath. When she opened her eyes, Ubukata's worried face looked down on her. He was safely buckled up in his command chair, while she had been allowed to sit down on the floor and lean against the bulkhead at his side, secured with an improvised belt glued to the ship body.

"Are you okay?"

"Yep."

He nodded and turned forward. There were more important things demanding his attention, like the flashing red lights on the engineer dashboard. Horus was already busy calling up screens, reports, detail views, and making the red lights stop flashing.

They remained red, though.

"Good job, Chief," the captain said. "We made it again."

"Sure, Skipper." He briefly glanced over his shoulder. "Will take some time to fix, though. If I gobble up enough spares, that is."

"Time enough for the collectors?" the pilot asked. Ubukata had introduced him as Philippe.

"Plenty," the engineer agreed.

"Do it," Ubukata said and leaned down to Syreen again. "You did better jumps before, I'm sure."

She rubbed her temples, still feeling somewhat dizzy.

"Sure. To be frank, I never did a three-sigma jump with damaged emitters before."

"Three? No, gal. I admit, it's only a five-sigma route, but—"

"She's right, Skipper." Philippe peered down on his panel. "It's a five-sigma route, but we did a three-sigma jump. Or, more precisely, we drained the capacitors as if for a three-sigma jump. For the rest, I must investigate first."

"That explains the strain, Skipper." Horus waved across his dashboard. "Lots of failures. I know the old lady isn't perfect, but I'd have expected her to do better. But what do you say about damaged emitters?"

Syreen placed her palms on the floor. "We jumped the planned hypervector, otherwise we wouldn't have arrived here. But we were insufficiently shielded against hyperspace, so it effectively became a three-sigma jump. Insufficient shielding can primarily result from three causes—firstly, from obstacles in the jump path, which we didn't have, secondly, from insufficient capacity, of which we had plenty, and thirdly, from weak or damaged emitters. As no responsible skipper would ever dare a jump with weak emitters, they must be damaged, and from the feel of it, I'd suspect the damage in the aft area—otherwise we'd be toast now."

The engineer called up more data. "Skipper, I don't know how she did it, but she's right. The log shows the emitters have been damaged in the aft—they broke upon entry." His fingers flew across the dashboard. "They were fine in the last inspection. Not new, but an acceptable standard. Should've held for a dozen more jumps."

Ubukata sighed. "Can you fix it?"

"I can fix some of them—but not all. Sorry, we're a few spares short."

The skipper sighed again. "I thought you'd bring luck to us. Seems we're stuck here until someone picks us up." He frowned at her. "My responsibility is clear. It can take a kilo-cycle before another ship comes along to pick us up. I must assure survival of my crew, and our emergency rations are limited. I can't share them with you, and I can't allow my crew to cut their own rations short."

CHAPTER THIRTY-ONE

Syreen wasn't shocked by Ubukata's decision, but by the brutal straightness he had communicated it with. It was effectively a sentence of death by starvation, unless she voluntarily left the ship through the airlock or cut her own throat. Obviously, he blamed her for the parts' sudden failure.

She nodded anyway. "Perhaps you're willing to grant me three last wishes. Firstly, I'd like to have a look at the broken emitters to see why they failed, if it's possible to tell. Secondly, I want to see how much repair is possible — after all, the remaining emitters still carried us here, so basically the ship can jump. Thirdly, allow me to calculate a solution for the next jump. If I can improve your jump by a sigma level, that might make good for the missing emitters. It's still your decision to jump or stay."

"You understand that your assistance will not earn you anything should I decide to stay?"

"I understand that I'm to die if we stay, while you might survive. However, you'd lose your ship, and the next one coming along might drop you on Appalahoo without jobs and few credits. They're not into welfare there, so you'd soon have to live off the country. You remember your potential neighbors?"

"They wouldn't . . ."

She nodded. "They would. Consider what they did to me, to a pretty girl — they quoted outrageous prices for room and food, unless I'd be willing to warm their beds. You don't have tits and pussy, so why should they waste their expensive imported food on you?"

Ubukata didn't like that line of thought, but couldn't come up with valid objections.

Syreen rose and patted his arm. "Let Horus and me have a look first, then I'll show Philippe my proposal, and after that, you consider your options again, okay? Right now, until we're done charging, you needn't worry."

CHAPTER THIRTY-TWO

Syreen gazed at the magnifying projection. The emitter casing showed numerous fine cracks. It was easy to tell they didn't belong there, but what had made the tough gear crack?

Horus almost knocked his head against hers when he stirred in the narrow maintenance duct, and his left elbow touched her right boob when he pointed at the emitter's rear end. "What do you make of that?"

She squinted. "What?"

He zoomed in and showed her a minor recess in the casing. "That."

"Oh. Molten?"

"Correct. With the emitter casing overheating and cracking, I venture a prognosis what we'd find inside."

"Toasted emitter."

"Right."

"But where did the heat come from?"

"Perfect question. Now let's have a look."

He pulled his arm back—again inevitably brushing her tit—and fumbled with the manipulator control. The magnified image changed and showed the place where the emitter had been mounted.

"See those lines? Power supply for aggregates farther behind. Shouldn't run down this duct—but the other one's impassable, after Philippe ran our shuttle against the hull and made a dent there. So when the lines needed refitting, the skipper decided to let them run here. In principle, not a bad decision, only . . ." Horus let the image turn. "See there? The clamp?"

She shook her head. "I don't see a clamp."

"Because there isn't one. Only those remnants—" Again he brushed her tit—"that show clear signs of brittleness. They didn't withstand the heat, the line came loose, landed on the emitter casing—well, you know the rest of the story."

"That doesn't explain why the other emitters failed."

"It does. Basically all those along this duct are affected. The old lady has four aft emitter ducts with twenty emitters each. If one fails, the others take the burden. However, when those others are also already overheated and overstrained, they will simply crack down the line. I'm sure if I check the logs again, I will find this one was the first, and the others following within microcycles." He tried to shrug. "Someone in the dock made a fatal mistake. Fatal for you, that is."

"You can't repair that line? Fix it back in place, so that it holds another jump?"

"I could, but what's the point? We're stuck here."

"But you have a few spare emitters."

"Four. I can't get this duct up with only four emitters. Even without overheating, they will fail the moment we jump."

"Twenty are broken here. What about the other ducts?"

"Should be okay—at least we don't have the heat problem there."

"So what if you take two out of all the other aft ducts, and one out of each forward duct? That would give you fourteen overall, and the remaining emitters should be able to take the little extra burden."

He paused. "That's daring."

"What if we go gentle? What if we do a seven-sigma jump?"

"*Seven*-sigma? Gal, nobody does seven-sigma jumps."

"I do them all the time."

She could sense his doubts and very gently radiated a little confidence. "Kasai trusted my calculations, too. You might at least give it a try. After all, this ship won't go anywhere soon."

CHAPTER THIRTY-THREE

Syreen patiently waited.

The captain looked at the calculation, then at Philippe, then at her, and then back at the numbers. "That's almost seven-sigma. Philippe?"

"I've rechecked the numbers twice. Everything fits — will be a very smooth jump. I'd bet on that."

"Yes." Ubukata looked at Horus. "How long do you need for the refittings?"

"Uh — I must be careful, so . . . a cycle per duct for extracting the emitters and checking them for damages. It's darn tight in there. And the affected duct — it's even tighter with the lines, I must see how I can work in there. Our automatic gear can't mount the improvised clamps. It must be done manually. That's easy, but crawling along that duct will take me a tencycle, and then I must find a way to crawl back — another tencycle. Only then can I send the crawler in to mount the emitters there, which will cost another tencycle or so. Even if I give up sleep, no less than four tencycles."

"And then we still don't know whether it will work."

"We must calibrate them — no deal — and run a deep check, and then we're ready to go."

The captain looked down. "Five tencycles at least, before we're ready to go. But you must sleep now and then." He shrugged. "That may not affect my decision. We're on emergency rations until we arrive at Woo. I'm sorry, Syreen."

She wouldn't survive five tencycles without food and water. They all knew that. There were worries, regret, but also

fear for life and determination. As crew, they had to stick together, and she was an outsider.

"I will mount the lines. I fit in the duct better than Horus,
and I'm sure I can mount those clamps. He can check my
work after. That way, he can extract the other emitters while
I'm working on the line. Worst case, I needn't crawl back until
we jump."

Horus shook his head. "Too hot. You'd be toast."

"That's why I said worst case."

"We'll do it differently. You go in with the clamps while I
retrieve the emitters. If everything works as planned, I'll be
able to send the crawler after you before you're all the way in.
The crawler can start exchanging emitters at the deepest point
and then work its way back while you follow. That way, we're
through within two tencycles—not counting your sleep
breaks."

"I can do without sleep for that long. What I need is water."

Horus glanced at Ubukata. "Skipper, if she's doing the
hard work for me, may I share my water ration with her?"

The captain rubbed his chin. "Water is not our problem.
Full ration for two tencycles. See that you get her out before
the lines go live again. Oh, and we cut down on showers."

"Thank you, Skipper."

Syreen gave a bow. "Thank you, Skipper."

"Make it work. We will all feel better if it does."

CHAPTER THIRTY-FOUR

Syreen didn't need much time to start cursing her offer. She had expected something like the maintenance duct she had visited together with Horus — with enough space to pass each other — but the actual cable and emitter duct was so tight that she had to struggle to move her arm over her head. She quickly discarded the idea of scratching her belly or anything like that.

Luckily, Horus had given her a jumpsuit so she wouldn't ruin her clothes — there were simply too many edges, sharp points or pinching cracks inside the duct.

Exchanging an individual clamp was no big deal. Making sure the cables sat where they belonged wasn't either. But in combination with crawling down such a tight, sticky duct and pushing her gear ahead, it was hard work.

It's for the mission. It's for saving this galaxy — and it's for saving my ass. It won't end here. See it like this — you didn't have a lot more freedom of movement in your skirmisher seat, and if you think about it, not a lot more in Assiduous' *seat. You can bear it.*

Now and then, she took a sip from her water container. *Next clamp, next move. Focus on the task.*

Soon she lost track of time. After a while, she heard a crackle in her ear. "Gal, how's it going?"

"All okay, Horus. This is clamp seventy-four."

"You're ahead of schedule, then. Great. I'm through with the aft ducts, extracted the second and last-but-one, and they're fine. Almost no wear, as it should be. I'm positive your plan will work. I owe you."

"Buy me a drink once we're on Woo."

"I'll try to beat the skipper to that."

She laughed. Such talk could make her momentarily forget about the situation, but her tummy was empty and didn't fail to remind her of the fact.

Traveling as star angel had its advantages, but also some disadvantages. She was tolerated aboard, but her legal status wasn't much better than that of organic waste.

She also had to consider that Ubukata wouldn't be the only one making the connection between the star angel and the bold corvette skipper. She should find a less conspicuous way to travel, and the sooner the better.

CHAPTER THIRTY-FIVE

Syreen followed Horus back to the bridge, still wearing her jumpsuit. She was hungry, tired, and also mentally worn-out, but she wouldn't withdraw into a lonesome corner now.

Horus reported, "We're through, Skipper. All emitters mounted and calibrated, the line is live, deep check done — all clear, of course except for the missing emitters, but even there, the diagnosis reports operational readiness."

"Oh — that's unexpected. What do you make of that?"

"There must be some redundancy in the equipment, and that's factored into the diagnosis protocols. The report recommends repairs at the next possible occasion."

"We will surely do that. So we're ready to jump, are we? Philippe?"

"We're at fifty percent and I have an updated solution for a seven-sigma jump in thirteen. Ready to go, Skipper."

"Do it, then. Well done." He turned to Syreen. "As you see, we were positive that your work would be done on time. No need to extend your suffering any longer than necessary."

She managed a weak smile. So he had begun acceleration to jump speed before they were even finished — for her sake, or because he had already lost too much time? Whatever it was, she had to be glad that he had at least included her fate in his considerations.

Thirteen centicycles later, the familiar feel of a transit comforted her. The jump solution left a little room for improvement, but the emitters had done their work well.

"Philippe?"

"Yes, Skipper?"

"I said, do it. When will we jump?"

"Oh—uh—we already did, Skipper." The pilot checked his dashboard. "Definitely, Skipper. This is the Woo system."

"I felt nothing."

"You shouldn't," Syreen chimed in. "With seven-sigma or better, the side effects are negligible, on people as well as on equipment."

Ubukata placed his palms together before his face. "Well. Words fail me to describe my relief. Initially, I was very worried about our fate—that's my only excuse for what I did to you. I can't make it undone. I can't make good for the fear of starving I placed in you."

"You did what you had to. You're the captain."

"I thank you for your understanding. Yet I owe you, for the ship, for my crew, for me. I will record another recommendation as star angel with the guild, but you deserve something more tangible. Either now or the next time we meet, I will fly the route you need, with or without cargo."

Now Syreen was lost for words. "I . . . uh, that's very generous of you."

"It's not. However, there's something more immediate I can do for you. Philippe, take care of the ship. Horus and I will treat our guest to a decent meal."

CHAPTER THIRTY-SIX

Woo Orbital wasn't half as large as Kyris, but twice as crowded. New ships docked every few cycles, others left. Most only stayed to pick up spare parts and provisions, few unshipped or transshipped their cargo or picked up local goods.

Syreen ambled the narrow corridors, squeezed past busily hurrying crews and crowded pubs, and mused about her next steps. Finding a ship wouldn't be a problem here, but finding the right ship—with the right route—could take time. As newcomers only docked for a short time, her best choice might have left before she learned about it.

She could ask the guild, and thus increase the risk of ruining her disguise, but she had decided upon arrival that Syreen, the star angel, would not appear on Woo. As for Syreen, the Duchy Fleet officer, and Syreen, the Navigator, those were entirely out of the question.

That wouldn't make her next steps easier, just the opposite. There would be only one role aboard a merchant ship she could assume. The crew had better be nice.

A few passersby gave her interested looks. She returned noncommittal smiles—she wouldn't let herself be caught soliciting. Not in a place where she was an illegal alien—well, she was as long as she didn't unveil her identity.

People might draw the right-and-yet-wrong conclusions anyway. With her shorts, sleeveless shirt and boots, she couldn't be mistaken—this wasn't the appropriate appearance for an officer.

There were very few visitors like her. In fact, there were few females at all, and those were wearing uniforms and were accompanied by several of their crew.

"Hello, my lovely lady."

The young man with a mustache, vest, and curly hair looked handsome and charming and smelled fresh, but radiated lecherousness — and hate?

Good looks, good manners, but her instincts said *Run!*

There was something deeply wrong with this young man. Syreen had no business with him, so she'd better send him away. She didn't.

She smiled at him. "Hello, Sir."

CHAPTER THIRTY-SEVEN

Syreen had to suppress a shiver when she sensed his victorious feelings. *Yes, you got me. But you have no clue who you got.*

"You must've arrived recently, or I'd already noticed you. Such beauty couldn't escape my attention."

"Yes . . . it's all so crowded here."

"Oh, yes. It's an old problem, and there's no way to fix it. Woo Orbital was designed far too small for the large number of people. Now it can't be expanded. But there are a few quiet places—if you'd like to join me?"

"I—I'd be glad."

He showed his teeth. "This can be intimidating if you're not used to such large crowds—where do you come from?"

"Appalahoo."

"Uh—where's that?"

He didn't know and she wasn't about to enlighten him. "Two jumps away."

"Oh, okay. This way, please. Allow me to lead."

She nodded and waved him forward.

"Apart from the crowd, do you like it on Woo?"

"I haven't been dirtside yet."

"Dirtside." He smiled. "You're a spacer, then?"

"I spent a lot of time in space, yes. Different ships, different stations. But I've been on planets, too."

"Where were you born?"

"Uh." The question took her by surprise—and hit a sore spot. "I don't know."

"How can that be? And your parents?"

"I don't know. I was found on a station. People took care of me and raised me." As a pilot, but he didn't need to know that.

"Oh. I'm so sorry."

She shrugged. "I get along."

"And you get around, don't you?"

She shrugged again. "That's part of it. Ships are meant to get around. We're getting around here, too, aren't we?"

"It's not much further."

Indeed, only a few corners away, he opened a door to a narrow side corridor without traffic. "A shortcut. The rear entrance of a very nice venue. The best forwine on Woo Orbital."

Syreen didn't sense truth. Instead, he radiated anticipation. She felt anticipation, too—her beast's anticipation.

He let her enter first. When she waited a few steps in, he just closed and locked the door behind them.

"Go ahead," he said.

She made two steps, paused, then walked on very slowly, hoping she'd appear insecure to him.

"Enough," he said.

She turned around, searching for another door. "Where? Are we there yet?"

"Your way ends here." He produced a short stick. A flick of his wrist produced the short humming blade of a vibrator knife.

She straightened herself. Her tongue licked her growing canines, giving a lisp to her words. "I don't think ssso."

CHAPTER THIRTY-EIGHT

With renewed strength, Syreen returned to the crowded corridors. This encounter hadn't brought her any closer to her mission goal, but she felt positive anyway. He wouldn't be a danger to other innocent young women ever again.

She closed her eyes for a moment. There were smells, noises, feelings—angry feelings, worried feelings, gloomy feelings, happy feelings, determined feelings. She didn't want angry, and probably couldn't score with happy and determined, but worried and gloomy might be the lever she needed. So she headed for a place predominated by these emotions.

The station's lower levels harbored the cheaper venues, easy to tell by the smell of poor forwine and greasy, spicy food. This was the place for those not spoiled by success.

Syreen considered following her gut feelings until she found out that these gut feelings were in line with the taste of emotions—some of the people had a bad taste, some tasted nice although gloomy.

She entered a rundown venue, squeezed her way through the people at the counter, picked up a forwine there, and moved on to the tables in the back, where she approached a table with five of six chairs occupied.

The man in the middle wore short gray hair all around his edgy face. The other four were all about her age and with hair of every other color—blond, red, brunette and black.

"May I?" she asked and pointed at the free chair.

"Sure," the old man said.

"I'm Syreen."

"Matt," the blond said.

"Ray," the redhead said.

"Bob," the brunette said.

"Jack," the black haired one said.

She waited.

"Homer," the old man said.

The four young men were busy admiring her. Homer was too worried to take more than brief notice of her. Syreen had to reach him. She focused on him.

"I can feel it—you're nice people. But you're worried. What can I do to make you happy?"

Answer me. You want to disburden your heart.

"We're stuck here," Homer said and stared into his glass.

Look at me and go on.

"We have cargo for Mongo, that's seven jumps from here. We'll be well paid once we get there, but we won't get there. Our navigator deserted us."

Syreen gasped. "Why—how can that happen?"

"We had a disagreement after the last jump. He had made a mistake—no big deal, but he wouldn't admit it. I couldn't let that stand. In the end, he gave in—or at least pretended to do so—and when we arrived here, he left us."

"Incredible. You can't get a replacement here?"

"Good navigators don't wait for a new ship on Woo."

"So what can you do?"

Tell me.

"I have no idea. I can't even transship my cargo—vessels usually arrive here full or almost full. If I can't deliver it, I must try to sell the ship."

"And fire your crew—here on Woo."

"Yes."

"I can imagine what that means. I'm stuck on Woo without a ship."

"Well—let me talk straight. I can't hire a ship's cat for a

ship without a navigator, but with your looks, you shouldn't have trouble finding another."

"Would you hire me as ship's cat if I found you a navigator?"

"Hehe. Nice try."

"No, really."

The captain folded his hands. "I'm in no position to turn a good navigator down—not even an average navigator. But if this is a scam set up by our nice friend, you better tell him to lick his own ass."

"I don't know him, trust me." *Trust me.* "My goal is to get away from Woo. If I can find you a navigator, I'd like to come along, so I'd share the risk."

"This could be a scam to get a team of two aboard. Pirates' accomplices, you know?"

"It's not. I despise pirates—if necessary, I kill them." *Forget my incognito, I could be stuck here for ages.* "Let me rephrase my last question—would you hire me as navigator if I found you a ship's cat?"

CHAPTER THIRTY-NINE

For quite a while, Syreen felt waves of emotions washing over him—disbelief, amusement, wariness, fear, hope, even anger.

When Homer calmed down, he said, "Now you're pulling my leg."

"I can see why you must think so, but your situation is too serious to make bad jokes about it. I am a qualified navigator."

"Can you prove it?"

"Here? I could tell you anything. But take me to your ship and I'll find you a fast and cheap route to Mongo. You can judge me by my results."

"Why should I even admit you to my ship?"

"Because you've got nothing to lose?" She smiled. "You can test me any way you imagine. I will answer you. But you know the true test is navigating."

"I still can't see how a ship's cat should know anything about navigation."

"Perhaps because you can't see why a navigator should have good looks? I know that few women other than ship's cats work for merchants, and I know why. But there's always the exception to the rule."

"Exceptions make me nervous."

"Indeed, and with your recent bad luck, you're entitled to be nervous. However, I badly need a ship but can't present my tac—that's why I tried to get a ship's cat job—and you badly need a navigator. We can help each other. You won't regret it."

He shrugged. "I fear I will. But in one point, you're right—
I have no choice. Come along."

Her own surprise was mirrored in the four younger crew
members. The captain had already risen and motioned them
to leave.

Docks looked mostly the same on any station, Syreen
mused. A corridor ended in a spacious room—probably large
enough to install passenger check-through facilities. Otherwise, there was just the hatch and the usual indirect lighting.

Homer pointed at the opening hatch. "The *Mary Of Skye*.
Welcome aboard."

Syreen didn't need to feel the hint of tension in him to
know this was a test. She wouldn't move as much as a finger
into the hatch before he did.

He waited, and she focused on him. "Skipper?"

The captain nodded and entered. Now she followed, casting a smile at the rest of the crew.

The hatch could use a clean and a paint, but she didn't see
anything that would indicate safety hazards. She wouldn't allow such on her own ship, but considering the size of a merchant in comparison with its crew, they probably had to set
priorities.

It didn't get better inside. *Mary Of Skye* was in dire need of
tidying up. But what could you expect on a ship with four
young men who probably still had to get to grips with their
jobs?

So she tried to ignore the stains and followed Homer to the
bridge. He stopped right behind the door and let her pass.

"There."

This was the second test. She headed straight for the pilot
desk, activated it and called up the navigation library. Luckily, the controls didn't differ much from *Narihiro's*—nor from

Raydancer's — so she had no trouble finding her way.

A flick produced a three-dimensional star map with Woo to her left and Mongo to her right. There were quite a few stars that would qualify as jump nodes — powerful enough for a recharge, distant from dangerous obstacles and thus easy to navigate, and some of them even had inhabited planets.

Syreen instantly saw a favorable, although not too easy course, covering the entire distance in four seven-sigma jumps. That wasn't the route Homer had mentioned though — he had spoken of seven jumps. Where would that take her?

She could look up past routes, she could look up high-frequented nodes, but that would be like cheating.

Homer stirred. She felt his impatience. Together with the rest of the crew he now stood in a half-circle behind her. She had to show them something soon, but first, she had to adapt the calculations so that they'd meet her standards.

So, what if I headed for this star — yes, past that, and here . . .

A moment later, the entire route appeared in the display. Visited stars were highlighted with their data, others faded. The jump characteristics followed. Three seven-sigma jumps, four six-sigma jumps. Not too bad either.

"Here you go, Captain."

The merchant stepped forward and gazed at her panels. "You didn't look anything up? I didn't see you check computer proposals?"

"Check my results first."

He grumbled and bent over the dashboard. A moment later, he stared into her face. "*Seven*-sigma?"

Her own gaze didn't waver, but she kept her mouth shut. The captain returned his attention to the data screens. Several times he paused, but didn't comment on her work. Finally, he turned back to her and his crew.

"Three seven-sigma jumps, and not one below six. But you don't go via Cirrus?"

"I promised you a fast and cheap route, Captain. Cirrus is

hard to navigate. But if you have business there, I will incorporate that into the plan."

"Oh, no. That's a very good route."

You bet. "It's not the best, though."

His brows went up. "No?"

A few commands produced the route she had discovered first. "This is the best."

The captain only briefly examined the new result.

"In private. Follow me to the galley."

CHAPTER FORTY

For once, Syreen had reason to be curious. What was the captain up to?

He didn't let her wait. As soon as they had reached the galley, he turned around. "You know your stars, of that I have no doubt. These routes are beyond compare. I respect that you don't want to tell me all, but if I want to trust my ship and my crew into your hands, I must know what a top-class navigator is doing here. You have a military education?"

She sensed his sincerity. "How did you guess?"

"Despite your daring appearance, your behavior is very disciplined—and I noticed how you looked at my ship. It's not up to your standards. No merchant would care about it, but you do. Why did you leave?"

"I didn't."

"But . . ."

"I'm no deserter. Events beyond my control brought me here. In order to fulfill my duties, I must travel on."

"I must be sure I'm not pirate bait."

"If I get any say in it, we won't meet pirates. That would only delay my travel—if they'd let me go. You know what pirates do with pretty girls."

He frowned. "Yes."

"So that's getting us nowhere. I can prove my navigation skills. There are some other skills I could prove as well. I'd qualify for ship's cat. I can't prove what I'm not. I'm no deserter, I neither collaborate with pirates nor with your former navigator, and I don't mean harm to your ship or your crew.

It's your call now."

"If I could only be sure . . ."

"You can't. One thing's for sure—without a navigator, you're stuck here. With me as navigator, you'll save plenty of time on the trip, you save money for maintenance and money for the crew."

Homer shook his head. "I will pay for your services. If I can't prove I have a paid navigator, I can't do the trip."

Syreen placed her hands to her hips. "But you needn't prove you have a paid ship's cat."

"Uh—but . . ."

"Did you watch your crew? Four healthy young men with healthy appetites, and I'm sure you're no eunuch either. They'd be terribly disappointed—as I would be, after I picked your table for your looks initially."

"For our looks?"

"Remember? I tried to sign up as ship's cat. That's what I had come for until I learned you need a navigator more dearly. I'd rather have kept the latter to myself—as it raises unnecessary questions about desertion and such. Yes, I'm still in for some fun. With all of you, together or in sequence."

And now I've got you by the balls.

CHAPTER FORTY-ONE

Syreen could almost see the wheels in Homer's head turn. He really had no choice, and he knew it.

She sensed his resolve first, before he reached out his hand.

"There's no life without risk. You're right—if it wasn't for the bastard who deserted us, I had no reason not to trust a good navigator. I will trust you. Welcome aboard, Pilot."

His grip was warm and firm. "Thank you. Your orders, Skipper?"

"Prepare ship for departure. We will leave as soon as we're cleared, and I will take care of that."

"Thank you, Skipper."

"Just a word—are you familiar with large and slow merchant ships?"

"I will not rip a hole into our *Mary Of Skye,* Skipper."

"Well . . . okay."

Syreen had certainly expected the large freighter to behave differently from *Raydancer* or *Assiduous.* Theoretically, she knew how a cruiser reacted compared to a skirmisher, but this was no simulator game, and she couldn't afford a mistake.

When her cue came, she checked the docking clamp signs—unlocked—and very gently pulled her stick. Nothing happened.

This was what her instructors had warned her about—*if you start moving a large, massive body, expect delayed reactions. Wait.*

She waited. A few slow breaths later, the computer

reported loss of contact to the dock — perhaps no more than the width of a hair, but they were free.

With closed eyes, she felt for the ship, the gentle humming of its magnetic fields, the surge of air, the elasticity of its body, and then she reached out and imagined their surroundings — Woo Orbital, its docking fingers, nearby ships and shuttles, the planet itself and the system's central star.

She's a good old lady, seasoned and tough. We'll get along together well.

She also sensed a little impatience in her captain.

Okay. Let's dance.

A firm pull at her stick, then a little twist of her hand, and the big body accelerated backward and began to turn around.

Easy.

This wasn't the place nor the time to show off. She didn't need to parade her cock. Risky maneuvers in combat situations were one thing. A merchant ship wasn't meant to give the pilot such an extra kick.

So they all needed a little patience until she had steered *Mary Of Skye* clear of Woo and its visitors and had her bow pointing system outward. Only then did she start acceleration toward a half light speed.

"Course for jump point set," she reported. "Data for first jump calculated and rechecked."

"Good job," the captain praised her. "Very smooth."

"Can't remember any better departure," blond Matt agreed.

"'Cause there wasn't any," black haired Jack added.

Syreen turned around and focused on her boss. "Thank you very much. I'm running on an empty stomach, though. May I ask you for lunch?"

"Sure," red haired Ray quickly agreed. "However, it's my turn for dinner now."

"That's fine."

Homer clapped his hands. "That's settled, then. Bob, you

have the bridge."

"Aye, Skipper."

Chapter Forty-two

Syreen checked her calculations once again. *Mary Of Skye* tended to drift to one side—her sub-light drive seemed to need recalibration. She noted that task for after the jump. As their jump point had moved, she had to adjust the jump parameters.

Nothing serious, but unnecessary.

"Ready for jump in ten, if you approve."

"Sure. Approved." Homer radiated relaxed confidence now. It had been a rewarding idea to join him for a special after dinner *dessert* in his cabin.

She entered his approval into the computer and leaned back.

The computer counted down the time.

There was a brief glimpse of vastness, and then her displays went blank.

She gazed at her dashboard. No data, no controls. Emptiness.

"I have a major malfunction here," she said aloud.

"Cancel jump," the skipper decided.

Syreen shook her head. "We already did."

"I didn't feel it."

"You hardly feel a seven-sigma jump, but we jumped."

"What did you do?" Homer rose and came toward her. "Step back from your station. Jack, come and have a look."

Syreen vacated her chair and withdrew to the bulkhead.

The chief engineer left his own station and walked once around hers. He probed the dashboard surface with two fingers and shook his head. "Dead."

Jack fetched a short tube from his right pocket and held it against a panel. It hummed happily. Next, he went on his knees and poked the desk from below, earning another hum.

Homer glanced at her, then at his engineer's back. "Jack, please. We're traveling an unknown system at fifty percent light speed. I need something."

"Working on it, Skipper." He opened a panel and reached up. A moment later, the dashboard screens lit up. "What does it read?"

"Restarting. Self-diagnosis," Homer read from the dashboard. "Controls — hundred, green. Scan — hundred, green. Engine — disconnected, yellow. Library — zero, red. What does that mean, Jack?"

"Nothing good, I fear." Jack closed the panel and rose. Next, he tapped the screen. "Engine reconnects, okay. Hyperdrive controller — green. Library — let me see. Star catalog — not available. Hyperspace catalog — not available. Navigation log — initialized. Backup catalog — not available, what the heck?"

"What exactly did she do, Jack?"

"Wait. I'll check the system log. Let me see. The last entry is the log access. Nav log initialization, engine reconnect, self-diagnosis, restart, that's all my doing. But here — *Nav library deep maintenance,* never heard of such a thing." He tapped once. "Discard star catalog — discard hyperspace catalog — copy to backup — override warning — purge system . . ."

The engineer turned away from the panel and faced his captain. "An attempt to wipe the entire system failed due to insufficient privileges. But the library is gone together with its backup. The automated command was issued by our recently departed friend, though. Kind of goodbye present, I'd say."

"You're sure she had no hand in this?"

Jack waved his hands. "Yes. Yes, skipper, from all I see

here, it was his doing, not hers. A delayed maintenance command, to be executed after the next jump. He failed at most points, but succeeded with the most important—the library."

"Which means—"

"We're stuck here. We have everything to move the ship around, but can't tell where."

Now Syreen dared to approach her desk again. "I should scan and decelerate now, Skipper."

"Oh. Jack, is that okay?"

"It is. The evidence can't be purged. I can make a log dump later."

"Well. Syreen, I'm sorry."

"Just let me do my job, Skipper."

"Oh, yes." He gave way.

She assumed her chair. Collision detector—nothing, okay. Displays came to life again, showing their vicinity, but without any data on nearby objects. She let the ship decelerate—there was still this slight drift, and she entered the respective correction, still under Homer's and Jack's watchful eyes. Next, she triggered a quick scan, unfolded the collectors, and then started the full system scan.

"Collectors?" Jack asked.

Syreen chided herself. *Military habits.* Merchants didn't recharge each time—they'd jump on as soon as possible.

"I reckoned we need some time to figure out what's happened and what to do next, so we might as well recharge."

"Oh—okay."

"We have another backup," Homer said. "It's in the office, next to the secondary log box. Ray, go and get it."

"Yes, Skipper!" The ginger-haired young man dashed off. A moment later, he returned, his emotions close to panic. "Skipper?"

Syreen could guess what he had found, and sent out a mental command. *Calm down.* She couldn't allow a freaking-out crew now.

CHAPTER FORTY-THREE

Not just Syreen, they all looked up when the captain returned, shaking his head with a sad face. "Gone. Did a thorough job, that bastard. Destroyed the safety chips, too."

"That's unheard of," Bob complained.

"I assume if it ever happened before, that ship was lost," Ray said.

"Not necessarily," the captain said. "You just have to wait for the next ship coming through the same system. On well-frequented routes, you have no problem."

Then he made a sour face and focused on Syreen. "Only, we didn't take the well-frequented route. Or is this a common spot?"

"No, it isn't," she admitted. "And we shouldn't even have reached it." Now she reported about the drift. "If I hadn't recalculated the jump, it might have taken us anywhere or nowhere at all. I can't check now, though."

"So we're fucked, right?" Jack said.

"No, we're not," Syreen said with determination. "Remember how I came up with my course? No lookup, no computer proposals. I'm a navigator. I don't need this stuff."

Homer shook his head. "You need the star maps, the charted obstacles, the calculations, and everything."

"It's all in here." She pointed at her head. "I memorized the stars and the jumps for our route. That's a safety precaution — if you end up in trouble, like with a pirate lying in wait for you, you can quickly jump on. Of course it's better to recalculate, and I'll do that. I just have to reenter the formulas into the computer — as I did before. Otherwise our computer would never have given us the data for a seven-sigma jump."

Now Homer smiled. "You know the entire formula set by heart — and the stars, and the jumps you had planned? That's unheard of, too."

She shrugged. "Navy drill, as you might have imagined. However, I was always good at navigation — best in class, to be honest. I will get us to Mongo. I promise."

Next, she patted Jack's shoulder. "But we should do something about the drift first, shouldn't we?"

Jack gave her a broad smile and stood straight. "Aye, Navigator, *Sir!*"

CHAPTER FORTY-FOUR

Syreen no longer marveled at her own ability to look at a star map once and remember almost every detail about it later. Other people could do the like inside a large space station, never ever losing their orientation—it was a different scale, but not really more complex, at least not as long as you didn't count the gradual changes over long periods of time.

She knew their route, and remembered the stars along it, but that wasn't all—when she closed her eyes and ignored noise, smell, and draft around her, she could hear them humming their slow song.

Syreen didn't need windows, scanners, or gravity sensors. Blindfolded and deafened, she could point not just at the central star but at many others in the close vicinity. When she put her mind to it, she could tell the respective parameters for a seven-sigma jump.

For a moment, she felt a pang—if she focused on it entirely, would she be able to sense her home world, the Duchy?

Not the place, not the time.

It wouldn't hurt to check her calculations with the computer's aid though. Juggling with too many numbers, doing all the calculations in her mind, was hard work, and prone to little mistakes with severe effects.

"Okay, guys." She flexed her fingers. "Are we ready?"

Homer gazed at his engineer. "Jack?"

"No more drift, Skipper. *Mary's* running straight. 'Twas that bastard's manipulation, too. I found proof."

"He'll pay for that. Once the evidence is registered with the guild, he won't get a foot on the ground anywhere." The captain nodded at Syreen. "Ready. Go ahead."

"Thank you, Skipper. I have a solution for a seven-sigma jump in four." She tapped the screen. "Transmitted. Our next stop is Moria Six, a mining colony. Prepare for jump in three."

There shouldn't be more delayed commands. Together, they had checked the system logs for suspicious entries. They had found how the bastard had done it, and what he had done. Many of his nasty commands hadn't worked—had failed due to a lack of privileges, as Homer and Jack had been quick to remove him from the system. He must have hoped they'd be more negligent.

The countdown reached zero.

Again, she sensed their transit, and then cast a wary glance at her panels. There was no failure this time, no deeply hidden script ghost haunting her controls.

She started the scan, checked her capacitors—almost full—and rechecked her calculation for the following jump.

Syreen turned to her skipper. "All clear."

Homer gazed around. "Already there? It's strange not to feel the jump."

"I could get used to it," Jack said. "Way less strain for old *Mary*—I'll go and check our sore spots anyway."

"Do that. Seems we're not running out of time soon, eh?" The skipper looked around and found no one objecting.

"If necessary, we could reach Mongo within the next cycle," Syreen agreed.

"Ah, but we don't want to tell the competition everything, do we?" Homer winked at her. "Moreover, we won't tell anyone we had a navy-trained navigator aboard. That's our secret, and keeping it secret is the least we can do to thank you for saving our asses, don't you all agree?"

Nods and acknowledgments came from all around. Combined with their grateful emotions, Syreen knew she had made new friends.

CHAPTER FORTY-FIVE

Syreen would have liked to relax with one of the men, but they were all way too respectful to even think of sex in her presence, and she in turn respected them too much to change their minds. So she felt a bit bored and lonely while slowly munching down her breakfast—which reminded her of the lack of sleep.

Should I find me a place for a nap? Their pilot must've had a bunk here—they just didn't show it to me yet.

Bob's brunette head peeked through the door. "Syreen? There's an incoming call from Moria Six."

"So what?"

"The skipper went to sleep. He said he doesn't want to be disturbed unless there's an entire pirate fleet."

"What about the others?"

"Asleep, too."

"So who's got the bridge?"

"Me."

"So why aren't you on the bridge?"

"Uh—but . . ."

"Get back to your station. I'm coming."

Before she could follow Bob, she cleaned up the remainders of her breakfast.

Syreen found Bob was sitting in his chair, a communication screen hovering over his dashboard.

"So. Who's calling us, and why?"

The cargo assistant waved to start the replay.

"*Mary Of Skye*, this is a distress call from Moria Six port authority. Receiving your transponder signal was a big relief. Please call us back—I won't leave my desk until you do."

"That's it?" Syreen asked. "He didn't say what he wants?"

"That's it," Bob agreed. "He wants us to call back."

"And what do you expect from me?"

He stared at her. "Uh—you're the pilot."

"Which means?"

Bob still stared.

"Bob, you know I'm no merchant pilot. Tell me."

"Oh." He sat up. "Sorry, I forgot. The pilot is the second in command. Only the skipper and the pilot can make decisions with regard to navigation and all. That's why I called you."

"Oh." *So I'm in charge now? Another responsibility I didn't explicitly ask for. Homer could have told me.*

"Okay. Give me a line."

"Aye." He tapped his dashboard and nodded. Another screen floated up to her.

She activated it with a flick of her hand. "Moria Six, this is *Mary Of Skye*. We received your distress call. Please specify the kind of distress you're in."

The round-trip delay should be more than a cycle. She had to be patient.

No.

I have to make decisions.

She went to her own station and sat down. Without the library, she couldn't even sketch a course to Moria Six—first she had to do another full system scan, enter the necessary calculation methods to derive planetary orbital trajectories from the two scans, and feed the data into a new temporary library.

Triangulating their own position was no big deal—that was something every ship had to do after a jump. However, for their ship it had only worked after she had taught the computer to do it without the library.

Only then could she set a fast course for Moria Six.

The engines' rising hum alerted Bob. "What did you do?"

"Set course for the planet. If I decide to help them, this will save us time, and if I decide to leave them alone, it won't hurt us."

"But . . ."

"But my scans didn't unveil any pirate fleet, so I'm in charge now, right? It's my personal policy to help people in distress as long as I can. Remember, that's how we came here."

That enticed a weak smile. "I understand."

"Good. Now that I'm on watch, could you fetch me a for-wine?"

CHAPTER FORTY-SIX

When the reply came, Syreen placed her cup down.

"*Mary Of Skye,* thank heaven for your reply. We had a mining accident. One of our people was severely injured five tencycles ago. We don't have the means for brain surgery here, and according to our doc, we can only keep him for so long in hibernation without permanent damage. However, the next message drone is due in nineteen tencycles, and ships come here about every three to four kilocycles — including our own. So I have no choice but to implore you to take him along to any destination with better medical equipment. We are at your mercy."

She glanced at Bob's frozen face. They both knew what merchant crews thought about picking up passengers — there was always the risk of inviting pirates in. A remote planet like Moria Six was the ideal pirates' hideout.

However, it wasn't the ideal place for an ambush on merchants — who'd want to lie in wait for several kilocycles?

"In hibernation," was all she said to Bob about it.

"Yes — but what will the skipper say?"

"If the skipper doesn't like it, he can relieve me from my duties as pilot and find another," she replied. "He shouldn't leave me in charge without specific instructions if he doesn't want me to act on my authority."

Syreen triggered her communication. "Moria Six, we've already set course for you. Expect our arrival and have the patient ready for shuttle pickup in four point three cycles. Other than that, we will not have any business on Moria Six and expect accordingly simplified procedures. I assume your company will provide reasonable compensation for live cargo to Mongo."

She muted her line and gazed at Bob. "I think you'll have to wake up Ray. He might need time for preparations."

"Ray?"

"He's the engineer responsible for live cargo, isn't he? He might know how to handle a hibernating person."

"Oh — sure."

I must not roll my eyes. This young crew still has so much to learn!

Another while and another cup of forwine later, the reply came.

"*Mary Of Skye*, thank you for your understanding and willingness to help. The patient will be ready for pickup, and there will be no formalities other than registering your visit. We would appreciate if you could take messages along. Regarding compensation — I can offer you little from the limited budget I am working on, but my company is registered with the guild, and I am authorized to issue a bill. Will you accept that?"

"Moria Six, we will accept the bill in good faith."

If Homer didn't agree with this, he could still deduct the amount from her pay — which they hadn't negotiated yet. What did a navigator earn, anyway?

When Ray appeared on the bridge, his face told of new worries.

"Hi Ray," she welcomed him. "What's the problem?"

"That passenger." He spat out the words. "We're no liner."

"No." She rose and faced him. "What would you do if you found another merchant stranded with a failed engine? Leave the crew behind?"

His eyes widened. "What? No, surely not!"

"As you know all too well, we were rather close to that

point—stranded with a failed navigation library. No liner would've come to pick us up, you know that. And no liner will ever come here, to this mining colony. Now you will stop questioning my decisions and do your job."

"But . . ."

Her glare made him stop. What were the sanctions for insubordination on merchant ships? Would it be a good idea to look up the rules before she had to justify her decisions to the captain?

Ray let his shoulders drop. "Where shall I put him?"

"As nobody bothered to show me your former navigator's bunk before going to sleep, you might as well put our guest there. I'll take my nap right here."

"Nobody bothered . . ." he echoed, and then made a face. "I guess we all forgot."

"Yes, you did. Well, I could have asked earlier. Now it won't matter much—I guess I won't have much time for a nap once we leave here."

Ray seemed to be waiting for something.

"What else?" she asked.

"What are your orders with regard to our guest?"

"Do everything to ensure his survival on our journey. You're the expert for livestock cargo, aren't you?"

"Uh, yes, but—"

"You know the specs for humanoid mammals. Temperature, climate, oxygen mix etc. If you don't know how to keep a person in hibernation alive and asleep, you have some time left to look it up—that's why I sent Bob to fetch you early. If you need further specifics, make a list and I'll ask them."

Basic officer training—don't let your team delegate tasks back to you. Make them use their own brains or get their stuff themselves. Offer a way to escalate specific questions, but no easy way out. Then step back.

Ray still didn't stir.

"Your task is clear?"

He nodded.

"Move your ass, then." She added a smile. "You can do it."

"Aye, *Sir*."

Chapter Forty-seven

Syreen woke up in her pilot seat and looked around. All green, no new messages, Bob was quietly watching her—what had interrupted her nap?

She sensed a bad mood approaching and judged that her skipper didn't agree with her decisions. That didn't surprise her.

Syreen wouldn't let Homer dress her down in front of the crew, but she couldn't undermine his authority, either. A public dispute was out of the question. So she reached out to calm him down.

When he entered the bridge, his immediate anger had vanished. His frown still didn't look promising.

Syreen rose and straightened. In her skimpy clothes, it was more of a parody than a true attention, but it should remind him of her navy heritage anyway.

"Skipper, a few cycles ago the bridge watch alerted me about a distress call from Moria Six. Bob also enlightened me about the formal line of command. With no specific instructions, I followed standard protocol and requested details. I learned about a medical emergency and, again in lieu of orders saying otherwise, I recognized the urgency and decided to help—as I before had decided to help you."

Her last words caught him on the wrong foot. She took advantage of his loss for words.

"You profited from the principles I act upon. Of course, I'm well aware of the risks of granting a stranger access to the ship—after all, as a young woman I'd be the one who fares worst in a pirate encounter. However, the risk a hibernating passenger could mean to us is limited, and I'm sure Ray already knows how to keep it that way."

Syreen could sense his resistance crumbling, and served her last strike. "They agreed to compensate us with a bill drawn on the guild."

Homer's eyebrows went up first, next the corners of his mouth twitched, and then he broke out into roaring laughter.

"Gal, you're a merchant pilot indeed!"

CHAPTER FORTY-EIGHT

The debate on who'd pick up their passenger had been short. Now Syreen was directing the shuttle down to Moria Six's spaceport.

Should anything happen to her, *Mary Of Skye's* navigation computer already held the data for the next two jumps. The second jump would lack fine adjustment and thus lose one sigma level, but would still safely take ship and remaining crew to Mongo.

She was the one to take the risk. If the entire accident story turned out to be a scam and Moria Six a trap, Homer would merely lose his temporary navigator, and the saving on her wages would help him buy a new shuttle.

"It's only fair," she had said. "I decided to take the risk, so I'm the one stepping into the line of fire. Moreover, that's the job for a navy pilot, isn't it?"

There was another argument she didn't mention — should anyone down on Moria Six play tricks, he'd volunteer for a blood donation.

She licked her lip. No, her canines hadn't grown yet, although she almost hoped for someone trying a trick on her. Her beast was always hungry.

What if she *persuaded* the authorities to forget registering her visit and took the opportunity to taste some samples — or even all?

That thought made her shudder, and she tightened her grip around the stick. Its shape and firmness didn't really help get her mind off those naughty imaginings, though.

The incoming call did help.

"*Mary Of Skye shuttle one, welcome to Moria Six. Please touch down on our shuttle pad next to the airlock and wait for us to extend the tunnel.*"

She flicked the comm switch. "Moria Six, roger, I'll be there in five."

Five centicycles later, Syreen triggered the comm again. "Moria Six, I'm awaiting your tunnel."

"*What – uh, already there? We didn't notice the touchdown.*"

"You shouldn't. I'm piloting a shuttle and not playing ball."

"*Tunnel is coming.*"

Syreen locked the controls, unbuckled, rose from her chair, and stepped to the airlock. Only after the tunnel had made contact did she open the inner hatch and enter.

The difference in pressure was minimal, so the outer hatch soon let her pass. She walked down the tunnel to the port airlock — both hatches were open there.

If they're so negligent with regard to even the most rudimentary safety precautions, no wonder they suffered a severe accident eventually.

A single man in a jumpsuit welcomed her with a hand wave, not without a smirk upon quick examination of her skimpy attire. She instantly liked his smile and his cleanly shaved head.

"I'm Lonny. Had a good flight?"

"I'm Syreen. Yes, very smooth."

"Smooth as your touchdown, what? Pussy feet."

"I prefer to spare my equipment unnecessary strain."

"Sure. You were the one who answered our call, right? Would you follow me to my office? Just the registration and the bill, and you're ready to go. Meanwhile, our doc will bring his patient. It won't take more than twenty or so — doc didn't want to take Aziz off the line earlier than necessary."

He led her toward a door.

"You're alone up here all the time?"

"Mostly not. It's more comfy inside—we only use the port when there's traffic. So please ignore the dust, I didn't clean up yet."

His office consisted of three chairs and a desk with a panel. Lonny tapped the panel and produced two screens.

"Registration—*Mary Of Skye,* independent merchant, guild roll ID, captain and owner Homer Parkinson, on its way from Woo to Mongo—an unusual choice of route, by the way, but of course we're glad—cargo not specified, that's okay, and you are Syreen—" He glanced at her.

"No surname, navigator."

"Navigator. Fine. Are you aware that our equipment didn't register your entry shock?"

"It was a smooth jump. Might be they didn't pick it up." They probably couldn't pick up a seven-sigma aftershock, but she wouldn't enlighten him.

"Okay. Well, that's it, would you please acknowledge?"

She did, and the screen disappeared.

Lonny pointed at the other. "Our bill, issued to your captain. You mentioned live cargo, and I applied the standard rate for a four-jump trip, is that okay?"

"I plan to do a two-jump trip. After all, it's an emergency, and we don't want to put any extra strain on our patient."

"Two jumps to Mongo? Isn't that risky?"

"Not at all. It will be a very smooth journey."

"I wasn't aware that there's such a route."

"It's the reason we came through here."

"Oh. Okay. I'll fix the bill."

He did so, signed it, and triggered the transfer. "Formalities done." Next, he pointed at a small symbol. "The train will arrive in eighteen. What can I do for you meanwhile?"

"You want to fuck me."

"Uh — what?"

"You want to fuck me." Syreen pulled down her panties. "Don't deny it. Don't ask questions. Just do it."

Don't worry. Other mental commands weren't necessary.

In the end, of course, he'd have to forget about the bite.

CHAPTER FORTY-NINE

"Prepare for jump in two."

Syreen leaned back in her chair and relaxed. After that enjoyable encounter with Lonny, four men of the colony crew had loaded the patient into her shuttle, and then she was off.

Back aboard *Mary Of Skye,* Ray had taken care of their guest, and she had returned to her pilot chair. A moment later, they were on their way.

She had cheated just a little. After accelerating from orbit around Moria Six, the optimal jump position was reached at forty-nine point eight percent light speed, and her modified formulas could take advantage of it.

As promised, it was a smooth jump. Homer didn't even comment on it, and Syreen simply waited for the results of the second scan to adjust and prepare their last jump.

"Ready for jump in one," she said.

"Go ahead," her skipper said.

A blink later, they arrived in the Mongo system.

"Well done," her skipper said. "The *Mary Of Skye* might be the first ship ever to do two jumps within a cycle—and most certainly we're the first ever to do a trip of four seven-sigmas. We owe all that to the best navigator ever. Thank you, Syreen. I will record my praise with the guild."

She took a deep breath. "What if I ask you not to?"

"Would you tell me why?"

"I'd rather not."

"As you wish."

"Thank you for the offer anyway."

"You're welcome. I'll call Mongo now." Homer called up his communicator. "Mongo port authority, this is *Mary Of Skye*, Captain Homer Parkinson. We have a medical emergency aboard — a patient with severe head injuries, picked up on Moria Six, in hibernation. I must ask for docking priority and immediate medical attention."

Syreen analyzed the scan data. The Mongo system was bustling with space traffic. She shouldn't have trouble finding another ship to carry her on — instead, she could afford to be picky with regard to the next destination.

Like most inhabited systems, Mongo had only one planet suitable for humans, and most of the traffic went there. Their scanners soon picked up the transponder and radio signals of three large orbital stations. It reminded her of the Duchy, and of the people who had died on the stations during the Association's raid, most of them civilians. *This bill is still to be paid.*

She drafted a choice of fast courses toward Mongo's orbit. Until she knew where to dock, she couldn't fix the details.

"*Mary Of Skye*, this is Mongo port authority, space traffic director Jupiter Konda. You are assigned to Sengele Station, dock five-four, and will be scheduled for priority approach once you advise us of your earliest possible arrival. A medevac team will be waiting at the dock to take care of your patient, who will be exempt from transit procedures. Standard docking fees apply."

Syreen felt Homer's gaze resting on her and touched her panel. "Okay, I have the station's transponder signal, and I have a solution for a high speed approach ready. Here it is."

"Go ahead," their skipper acknowledged, and she triggered their engines.

"Mongo port authority, prepare for *Mary Of Skye's* arrival as follows." He passed her data on. "Be assured that our pilot won't miss her target by as much as a finger. Bets are accepted."

After he cut the line, she smirked at him. "Bets?"

"The Mongo people love betting," he said.

"Count me in with four, Skipper," Jack called. The others quickly agreed.

"What does that mean?" Syreen asked.

Jack turned to her. "I'm joining in with my full pay for the last four legs. If we lose, it's all gone, but if we win, I profit according to my share of the total."

"Oh. Well, it's a safe bet."

"We know that. They don't. The reward will reflect that."

"You want to join in?" Homer asked her.

"I would—do I have any pay to bet?"

"You were hired as navigator. You get a navigator's pay."

"In that case, all of it."

Which means I won't take a nap now but watch Mary and make it happen for sure.

CHAPTER FIFTY

Syreen felt exhausted, like someone who'd stayed too alert for too long — which was exactly what had happened. But she hadn't rejected Homer's farewell invitation.

Now he watched her over the rim of his mug as she raised her own beer to clink with his. He smiled and took a long draft.

"I'd understand if you prefer not to tell me where you're going next," he began. "However, the more you ask around, the more people will learn about you and your destination. I know some of the skippers here — met them before, transshipped trades, exchanged crews, and all — and can tell which routes they were taking last time. So, if you would trust me enough, I could direct you to the skipper you need — and could recommend you to him, so he'd take you along. It would be your call how I should introduce you, as my navigator or my ship's cat — whatever you like. I'd really appreciate if I could be of at least some assistance to you, after you've done so much for us."

She sensed his sincerity. "Will you find a new navigator on Mongo?"

"Oh, sure I will. Never of your quality, sure, but there's a functioning job market. The truly large ships pass through here, too, you know? The ones that employ two navigators. Eventually, junior navigators become seniors and find their own ships, or they stay aboard and the senior looks for a new challenge — or a less demanding schedule. Either way, they'll be attracted by a ship that can be navigated as precisely and easily as our *Mary Of Skye* — plus the challenge to integrate the new library."

Which will probably wipe out my coding. Can't help it.

"Well. You're right — I'd prefer not to tell anyone where I'm going next, but you're also right that your assistance will make things easier. My destination is Nysa."

He watched her for a while, drank from his beer, and wiped his mouth. "Nysa, eh?"

She nodded.

"The heart of Associated Planets. You're in their navy?"

"No." As an afterthought, she added, "You don't like them."

"Bullies, all of them. Started a few kilocycles ago. Their warships appeared everywhere, making undue demands, harassing honest traders, interfering with everything. People bit their tongues, swallowed their anger, refrained from complaining — or were shot, just like that. Not with the large star nations, oh no, they knew where to draw the line, but arrive at any smaller system and you suddenly face a battlecruiser asking you to stop and heave to."

"Which technically makes them pirates."

"Bite your tongue, especially as you want to travel there. Anyway, I'm glad you're not one of them, I can't imagine what your business with them is, then."

You needn't know that.

"No matter. I checked a few names before I brought you here. They might even show up for a beer later. The man you need is Captain Amos, Pierre Amos. His *Stormwatch* regularly travels to Eiffel. That system is one of the Association's main hubs, so you shouldn't have trouble finding a ship to Nysa there."

"Sounds good." She sensed some reservation in him. "Or not?"

Homer frowned. "Well. He's a ... uh, well, let me put it like this, he's a womanizer. He might have a ship's cat already, and even as navigator, you might not be safe with him."

Syreen nodded. "I can't afford to be picky, not even after our little bet." Which had tripled her pay and given her a quite comfortable budget—unless she spent it on extravagancies like a passenger ticket. "Remember, I'm prepared to be hired as ship's cat, so I don't expect to be safe."

"Er—uh—yes. That's how it is, isn't it? But as navy pilot— it's a shame that a woman should be forced to do this."

"I'm not forced. I could find another way, hire myself as navigator, steal a ship, or travel as a blind passenger with livestock cargo. Whatever. I could neglect my duty and stay away. I'd find another job. No, I'm not forced."

"You're not the usual ship's cat."

"No. Okay, it's a shame if there's no other way for women to earn a living—but who says so? If the rules of the game don't let you win, change the rules. Get in charge, kick some ass, prove you're the stronger gender. A pair of balls doesn't establish leadership."

"Easily said."

"Yes, I know. Males quickly take advantage of weak women. The strongest survive, law of nature, and all. But weak males can be taken advantage of as easily. Grab them by their balls and lead them around. A strong woman can use her pussy to get everything she needs." She thought of *Assiduous,* of her ship's pilot seat, of his truly big cock. Using her pussy, she could direct the living ship like no other pilot could control any other ship, and could experience sensations no other pilot could understand.

She'd take advantage of Mr. Amos in more than one way.

PART TWO—TRAP

CHAPTER FIFTY-ONE

Syreen ducked under Captain Amos' glare.

He waved a hand toward the galley. "Why don't you make yourself a little bit useful and clean the floor? I don't know why I took you along."

Yes, you know well enough. For my tits, my ass, my pussy and my tongue.

She dared to look down on her not yet finished plate.

"You can finish lunch later. Now get down to work."

Syreen pushed back her chair, rose and walked over to the galley, where she picked up a vibration cleaner and knelt down.

"See that ass? That's the way I like it most."

"Except for the shorts," Marv, his pilot, argued.

"Right. Syreen, would you be so kind and pull them down?"

She turned around long enough to show them her erect middle finger, and both men laughed.

When both men had left the mess, she picked up her by now cold meal and reheated it. The process didn't improve its taste, but didn't do it major harm, either—she was accordingly careful in her choice of food.

Now she had to be quick. She had just managed to finish her dish when the call came. "Crew, prepare for jump in two."

Syreen's nausea faded quickly—she didn't like Marv's five-sigma jumps at all, but personally, she could cope with the side effects.

She knew that the hyperspace they passed through was smooth enough to jump at seven-sigma. She sensed it. There were no obstacles around. Marv was simply too lazy to refine his solutions, and his skipper didn't care about the extra wear it meant for the emitters.

It was time to clean the table.

Not much later, her skipper leaned through the door. "It's time."

"Sure, Skipper." She shook her hip and followed him to his cabin. After the jump, as soon as he had recovered and had nothing to do, he liked to relax.

He unpacked his cock even before the door closed behind her. She went on her knees and started to suck until it had grown hard, then rose and pulled her shorts down.

"Turn around and bend over," he said.

She simply smiled and pushed his chest hard, so that he fell on his bunk backward. He wheezed. Next she mounted him, firmly grabbed his erection, and lowered herself down on it.

"Oh, gal!" he moaned.

"Hush." She began moving her pelvis and leaned forward, down, toward his throat.

His hands were on her buttocks.

Her fangs dug deep. Their lustful emotions joined. That was the true taste of passion!

When Syreen entered the mess again, Viggo, the engineer, and Marv smiled at her. She sensed their mix of envy and excitement.

Marv rose. "Alone? Where's the skipper?"

"The skipper needs some rest now."

"But you don't? Why don't we . . ." He rocked his pelvis.

She pointed at his crotch. "I'm so . . . *wide* now. Do you think you can satisfy me anyway?"

"Babe, I'm a rock. You'll never want to feel anything else again."

"I doubt that." She winked at Viggo. "Don't go away. I'll be back soon."

Viggo grinned.

Marv made an angry face and grabbed her firmly by the arm. "I'll show you."

She let herself be pulled away, but not without showing Viggo a last cheeky smile through the door.

The pilot pulled her into his cabin, tossed her with her back to the wall and pressed both her wrists to the sides of her head. "I'll show you."

He forced his lips on hers and his tongue into her mouth, pulled her wrists further up to hold them with one hand, and then fumbled with his pants. His erection pressed hard against her naked thighs. When he failed to pull her shorts down with one hand, she lifted one leg to the side, thus inviting him to feel her wetness up there.

Marv quickly followed with his cock. Once he had penetrated her, his now free hand reached for her tits.

Syreen returned his parody of a kiss with her own ravenous power, and when the opportunity came, she firmly bit his tongue.

"Ouch!" He pulled back and let her left tit go, probably to smack her.

Next, she sank her fangs into his throat.

CHAPTER FIFTY-TWO

With her recent journey already fading from memory, Syreen ambled along the corridors of another busy space station. Different in smell, lighting and emotions, but similar in layout and purpose, and yet, there was one aspect of Eiffel Seven that continued to disturb her.

It was the fact that it belonged to the Association, the same star nation that had come to her home and shot all the Duchy's space stations without warning, indiscriminately killing soldiers and civilians aboard.

That was the kind of crime which might raise the other star nations' ire, which might make them collaborate against the culprit—if someone could gain their attention and make them overlook the fact that Associated Planets commanded one of the largest and powerful navies in space, with obviously well-maintained dreadnaughts and battle cruisers, and crews who knew how to run them.

Were other nations prepared to challenge and defeat them? Were they able to fight them—assuming they were willing?

Syreen was sure that even if they might listen to a mere lieutenant, only circumstantially field-promoted to Fleet Commander in Charge, they wouldn't bother to take action just on her word.

She needed evidence—aside from the atrocities committed to her home planet—and explanation. Why had the Association acted? What were they up to? Trying to gain military advantage way above what they already commanded, trying to get their hands on the ancient weaponry of a long-forgotten race, but why and to what end? If she could retrieve such evidence, people would listen to her. If she could provide such evidence along with the visible proof of such an ancient device's existence . . .

That proof was far away, hidden in the remote area of some backwater mining planet, and couldn't help her here and now, just like Captain Amos wouldn't help her here and now.

She hadn't told him of her next destination when she had made him hire her as ship's cat, and she hadn't asked him when she had left him and made him forget her. He had no need to know.

Syreen now had to find out which ship, which skipper would travel on to Nysa, and then make him take her along. Preferably he'd succumb to her charms and looks. If not, she had her ways.

So deeply lost in her thoughts, Syreen almost ran into another man who stopped in her path to look something up on his tab.

At the last moment, she stopped and fought for her balance. "Oops."

The man looked up, took in her appearance — sleeveless top, shorts, boots — and smiled at her. "Oh, hey!"

"I'm sorry."

"Oh, no, I must apologize. I was blocking your way — wasn't watching others when I checked my destination."

"I was lost in thoughts, too."

He scratched his chin. "Were you? Uh — may I be of any assistance? My name is Cherry, Neville Cherry."

Neville looked sweet to her, and his emotions tasted nice, too. A cherry indeed, perhaps worth a taste?

"I'm Syreen. Nice to meet you, Neville."

"Syreen — just Syreen?"

"Yes."

"How uncommon. Anyway, may I invite you to a glass of forwine and then repeat my offer?"

She put on her most enticing smile. "You may."

Syreen would have expected anything from a rundown speakeasy to a secluded love nest, but not the classy restaurant Neville led her to.

The entrance was guarded by a tall man in uniform with epaulettes, golden buttons and linings—a parody of the AP admiral she'd met before. Her skimpy attire seemed to be quite out of place, and the guard's disapproving gaze confirmed her impression.

However, as Duchy skirmisher pilot she had learned to appear like a true officer even when naked, which she could do with the same stern ease when dressed. She paired it with the glare she reserved for insolent recruits. The guard shrank by about three fingers and botched his imitated salute when she passed him.

Neville radiated surprise, approval, and joy. Had this been a kind of test? If so, had she passed, and more importantly, had she given herself away by passing?

No. From the little he'd seen, Neville could tell she was not just a cheap floozy, but no more. Walking tall and staring down door guards was not a trait reserved for officers.

So she continued her act inside the anteroom, radiated confidence and pride that contradicted her attire, made it appear like a deliberate attempt to dress down, and from the feelings she sensed, the staff bought into it.

As did Neville, who treated her with cautious respect and not at all like the ship's cat she appeared to represent. This was a nice change after her last skipper, so she let it happen.

They passed the doors to a bar on the right and a fine restaurant to the left—did he plan to take her to a secluded booth? But then he turned right and indicated to her to enter a room with small tables—obviously dedicated to customers who didn't plan to dine.

He let her choose a table, sat down after her and then called a waiter to order two forwine.

Only when the forwine had arrived and Syreen had taken the opportunity to taste it did he repeat his offer.

"You were lost in thoughts, you said. May I assist you in finding your way out, or in any other way?"

"Maybe. I'd like to learn about ships departing soon."

"Travel agencies are located on level two. But that's not what you mean, do you?"

"No. Merchant ships."

"Merchants don't take passengers along."

"But crew."

"Ah. You want to be hired—um, as I heard, that's rather uncommon for young women."

She shrugged. "It's not."

"Only for a certain type of woman."

"Yes."

"Uh—I mean—well . . ."

"Leave it. What are you doing on Eiffel Seven, other than inviting young women for a forwine, Neville?"

"Me? I'm a hardware sales rep. My company deals in pots, pans and dishes, cutlery and all the stuff restaurants and bars need—or merchant ships. So I'm indeed able to help you. The port authority keeps a list of ships, incoming, docked or in the roads, outgoing—it's public, but you must know where to look for it."

"So I can just go to an information booth and look it up?"

"If you don't want to call it up on your tab, yes."

"I don't have a tab."

"Not? But . . ."

"I'll change that soon. I assume the shops here claim

reasonable prices, unlike during my previous stays."

"If you're looking for cheap one, take a Quickpad. If you prefer value for money, take a Masterpad, where the cheapest model will probably do. Both are locally produced and won't cost you a fortune." He leaned forward. "Let the shopkeeper show you the ships-in-port list as demonstration, and you have the link you need."

"Will the list show any detail about the ship and crew?"

"Sure. Size, skipper, cargo, all registration details, as it comes in. Port of destination, once it's set, maintenance polls, crew wanted—however, certain vacancies are not advertised."

"Of course not." She took a sip and smiled. "You're very helpful, and the forwine is excellent. Is there anything I could do for you in return?"

Neville shook his head. "No. From what you told me, you're unemployed, hard pressed for credits, and willing to do a *job* other women wouldn't consider even if they were desperate. I cannot and will not take advantage of your situation."

Now Syreen leaned back and opened her arms. "You don't like what you see?"

"I do. You're pretty and kind. You could be my daughter, and I wouldn't want to see my child in your situation ever. So—no."

"Well, okay." *In return, I won't take advantage of you, although you'd surely taste sweet.*

CHAPTER FIFTY-THREE

Syreen checked out some tabs before opting for a tough and compact new model, not the cheapest, but indeed good value for money, and after a quick demonstration of the ships-in-port list, she left the shop for dinner — with a little detour.

One of the recently arrived merchants, the *Easiness of Low Aspiration,* or for short the *Easiness,* under command of the honorable Captain Dar Ki Bhannain, had accepted freight for Nysa and would soon depart. She'd check him out. Hoping he'd treat himself and perhaps some of his crew to a decent farewell dinner, she waited to intercept him at the junction from his docking corridor to the central ring.

Three times, she used her mental skills to distract patrol men who were looking for undesired women soliciting. Five other times, she had to get rid of undesired johns.

Finally, a group of four people approached through the corridor, and one wore the sleeve stripes of a merchant captain. She withdrew into another doorway and let them pass. Keeping some distance, she then followed their emotional taste.

They soon entered a bar that Syreen's new tab identified as mid-priced and as accepting table reservations. She quickly added her own reservation and followed.

The venue employed its own guard, which she passed with the same ease as the one before. Inside, she mentioned her reservation to a waiter, added a smile, and earned one in return.

"Follow me, please."

Her table was close to the bathroom doors, under a large video tank, loud and uncomfortable, but she had her own table, and from there, she could watch the *Easiness'* crew.

She thanked her waiter, still smiling, and then browsed the menu for a healthy meal.

Most merchant crews were all-male, most were straight, and most men felt the call of nature on those long hauls. That had to be the reason why ship's cats weren't uncommon and generally accepted, and that was the reason why the *Easiness'* crew would be vulnerable to Syreen's bait.

They weren't the only men casting occasional glances at her during her dinner, but she discouraged others by a disapproving glare or, if that wouldn't suffice, a gentle mental push.

It's easy, almost too easy.

However, when her designated victims failed to make their next move, she had to take action.

She rose, walked across to their table, and leaned forward toward their captain. "Skipper, folks, I couldn't fail to notice the attention you spent on me. You might have considered my possible acceptance of an indecent proposal, as I had considered the likelihood of receiving such a proposal soon. Well — your assumptions were correct, I am indeed inclined to join your crew on your next trip, which will give you plenty of opportunity to try out my skills. By the way, I'm Syreen."

"Syreen." The captain scratched his long, gray beard. "Yes, I see what you mean. However, you must know, it's my company's policy not to allow ship's cats aboard."

"Why?"

"My company regards this kind of employment — using women as sex workers — as humiliating and dishonorable. Such behavior should be discouraged. I agree with that, of course."

"Of course." She leaned a bit more forward. Her shirt front

hung loose, displaying the view of her tits. "You are right. I wouldn't wish on any woman a situation where she'd be forced to accept a job as sex worker. However, banning the role of ship's cat is only the first step. Is your company ready to do the next step?"

"Which next step?"

"Hiring skilled young women for regular jobs, like apprentice engineer, assistant cargo master, junior navigation trainee."

"Women wouldn't want such a job."

"Why?"

"There are pirates, and when they find female crew . . ."

"Granted. But that's every woman's own decision. As ship's cat, that decision is made for them." *While you're still horny, and your gaze is still firmly fixed to my cleavage.*

She granted him a moment to digest her statement, before she added, "You might profit from a junior navigation trainee. I'd accept working for marginal pay, do all regular duties, and during my time off, I'm still open for honorable social interaction of any kind."

"Uh—but that'd be . . ."

Now she reached out, placed a finger under his skin, and whispered, "Don't assume you're the only one who's oversexed and underfucked here." *And hungry for the next bite.*

CHAPTER FIFTY-FOUR

"Come here."

Syreen was squatting before the engineering dashboard. Now she looked up at Kaname, the *Easiness* pilot. He had pushed his chair back and clapped his upper legs with both hands.

Chief Pekka nodded and thus released her.

She went over to Kaname to ride on his legs.

"No, have a look at the plot."

She turned.

"Did you ever see a hyperjump calculation before?"

"Yes."

"Indeed? Remarkable. Okay, in that case, tell me what you think about our next jump."

In general, she trusted Kaname to do his job. Unlike her last pilot, he did thorough and detailed calculations, aspiring to the highest possible sigma level—as far as his software allowed. Rewriting the code for seven-sigma calculations was beyond his duties, though.

Syreen leaned forward and checked the displayed trajectory with its data. She didn't like what she saw. "That looks like a rough jump. Only four-sigma?"

"Wow, that was quick."

"The computer told me." She pointed at the respective data.

"You knew what to look for."

"Sure. That's the one number telling me how sick I'll feel."

The chief engineer laughed out loud. "Trust that girl to

know what's important and what's not."

Kaname gave a brief laugh, too. "Okay, Syreen. If you're so quick-witted, can you tell me what's wrong with this jump?"

That was easy, too, but she examined the rest of the panel before she answered. "It's passing too close between these two stars. It's difficult to calculate a safe route around obstacles in hyperspace. That's why ships do multiple jumps between two destinations. Now, that next star is not a destination, it's just a waypoint toward Colossus, and it's not the best possible waypoint."

The pilot leaned forward and close to her. She could feel his breath at her ear. *"That* is extraordinary. What would be the best possible waypoint then?"

She pointed at a different star, quite some distance away from the straight route. "That one. No obstacles."

"That one? Now that's far from obvious. Let me see." The pilot entered some commands, and the computer produced some draft solutions for the two jumps. "Bite me."

Later.

"What did she find?" Chief Pekka came over to them.

"Two super-smooth six-sigma jumps, just outside the usual proposal corridor. And if you look on the plot, it's there in plain sight. Trainee Syreen?" He gave her a slight push.

"Yes." She rose and stood straight between his legs, her chest rather close to his face.

Kaname looked up at her. "You deserve formal praise. I daresay you could really become navigator, not just for the records."

She curtsied. "Thank you."

"And now — would you want to try refining that solution?"

In a way, she felt torn. By improving the draft, she'd give even more of herself away. However, it wasn't just an offer but a request — a request she couldn't deny. She *was* a navigator, and every suboptimal jump made her itch.

"Sure."

His hand rested on her thigh when she started entering commands. She did it by the Books, just the basics, but she also knew where she wanted to arrive. So it didn't take long before she could present her result. "Here."

"Better?" Pekka asked.

The pilot remained silent and examined the data, shook his head, examined it again, pulled up another screen and ran a few checks, then wiped his data away and turned to the engineer.

"Better. Far better than anything I could have done."

"What do you mean?"

"Pekka, from what I see here, she's the navigator, and I'm the trainee. I've got the experience of a lifetime, and she outdid me like it's nothing."

"She's got a run of luck then?"

"No."

Suddenly, she felt his arms around her, pulling her tight, and then he kissed her neck.

"Sorry," he whispered. "Couldn't hold back." Turning to the engineer, he went on, "You don't enter the specific parameters by luck. You don't know which commands to trigger by luck. She knew what she was doing. Didn't you, Syreen?"

That wasn't what she had intended. Obviously, her attempt to veil her talent had failed. *Okay, damage is done.*

"I knew," she admitted. "After all, that's what I was hired for. With your company's laudable policy, you didn't think I'd just cheat my way aboard, did you?"

Her mocking voice made him laugh, but then, he said, "To be honest, I did think so. I wanted it so, because you look too cute to miss the opportunity to make love with. And that's why I wanted you to be a ship's cat."

"I want to be a ship's cat now, too," she purred. "You just saved a lot of time on that calculation. Will we celebrate it?"

He rolled his eyes. "Pekka, can you take the bridge?"

"Sure. Unless you want to do it right here . . ."

Kaname shook his head. "The skipper wouldn't approve of that."

Syreen reached one hand out to the engineer. "But you'd like to watch us."

The chief's face turned red.

She laughed, and then Kaname lifted her and carried her away.

CHAPTER FIFTY-FIVE

The *Easiness of Low Aspiration* left hyperspace smoothly, and Syreen felt a sudden urge to purr. She quickly suppressed it.

Captain Bhannain cleared his throat. "Well done again, Kaname. I'll commend you for a bonus for finding this route to Colossus. It will save the company a lot of money."

The pilot gave a bow. "Thank you, Skipper. I must, however, decline your offer, as the last two jumps were not my doing. As a responsible pilot, I checked and approved them, but the credit must go to the crew member who found and calculated both jumps—our junior navigation trainee Syreen."

"You mean, she assisted you?"

"No, Skipper. I showed her our usual jump—always been a pain in the ass—and asked for her opinion. She pointed out that it's poor, why it's poor, and asked why we did it. I asked her what she'd do—and you've just experienced her solution. Again, she did not assist, she did it all by herself. I only watched her working by the Books."

"If she did it by the Books, why didn't you see that solution before?"

"Because it's slightly more outside the straight way than we'd normally look for. Okay, that's not in the Books, but it isn't against the Books either."

"You mean she didn't pick a different proposal, but came up with her own route?"

"Yes, Skipper."

"Extraordinary. Syreen, how did you find that route?"

"I looked at the star map. It appeared less dense that way. Of course, I could have missed other obstacles, but the computer would have told us. This area is very well charted."

He scratched his beard. "I've never heard of a navigator who found a double six-sigma route just by looking at the star map. You, Kaname?"

"No, Skipper."

She felt the captain's gaze resting on her, and she felt his mixed emotions.

"Why did you sign up as junior navigation trainee, Syreen?"

"Because you wouldn't have taken me as ship's cat, Skipper."

"No — why didn't you sign up as navigator?"

"Because you wouldn't have taken me either. Nobody would have, not until I could prove myself useful. The usefulness of ship's cats is more obvious."

"She has a point there, Skipper," Chief Pekka chimed in.

"Hum — yes. In any case, I judged this double jump worth a bonus, so you should receive that bonus. There's a difficulty, though — the company will not pay much bonus to a junior trainee, regardless of the gender. If I assume right, you put no particular value in our company's praise, do you?"

"Not really." *Not at all. The fewer people who learn about me, the better.*

"If Kaname claims the bonus and passes it on to you, you're better off with regard to credits. The downside is, it won't help you to get a job."

Syreen shrugged. "Praise or not — how many skippers will hire me as a navigator? I can't change the fact I'm a woman."

"Not many will, admittedly. However, I will pass the word around among my colleagues." He gazed at his pilot. "Kaname will receive the praise for spotting your talent. This won't hurt his reputation either."

CHAPTER FIFTY-SIX

After a hearty breakfast, which Syreen had enjoyed together with the entire crew, Captain Bhannain waved in her direction. "Would you try to calculate the next jump, too?"

She quickly put down her cup. "Of course, Skipper. That's my job as junior navigation trainee, isn't it?"

And to the abyss with my cover. I'm just not made for this kind of role playing, not with such honest merchants.

There was still time to change her approach once she reached Nysa. Now she had an immediate task to solve.

Or not quite immediate—Kaname had to finish his breakfast first. So she leaned back and closed her eyes.

A solitary presence sang its song only to her mind. Slowly pulsating, rotating, gravitating, radiating, in tune with its fellow stars, oblivious to the bustling wildlife on its only planet. It felt so different and yet so familiar.

A dissonance pulled her from her quiet trance. Something had pierced the wall between the planes. Downward.

She opened her eyes. "We have a visitor."

The captain sat up, a napkin in his hand. "What visitor?"

A moment later, *Easiness* sounded a chime.

"Arrival," he said and tossed the napkin aside.

"I'll check." Kaname jumped up and hurried toward the bridge.

"How could you know?" the skipper marveled before he followed his pilot.

Yes, how could I know? I won't enlighten him.

They all gathered on the bridge. Syreen retreated to her corner, but Kaname quickly waved her forward. "Come. This is part of our job, too."

So she joined him at his dashboard.

He produced some diagrams. "A light aftershock. That's good. You know why?"

"Smooth jump, or a small ship." She glanced at the figures. "A jump can hardly be that smooth." *Unless I do it.* "So it must be a small ship — much smaller than a freighter. Military."

"Correct. Can't be a pirate. That's good news."

"More or less," their captain grumbled. "If they don't decide to delay us."

"And if? We have nothing to hide." Syreen looked around.

"You're right — more or less," Bhannain repeated. "Sorry to unsettle you, but they're not always considerate, especially with regard to ship's cats — and they'd see you as such, whatever the records say."

"Then they better not come here. Or if they do, they shouldn't find me."

"You can't hide from them. If they're serious, they send sniffers into every duct."

"In that case, it's probably better they find me somewhere — but out of your sight, so you don't feel inclined to interfere. You couldn't help me anyway. Better you don't know."

Her last remark created an awkward silence.

155

CHAPTER FIFTY-SEVEN

Syreen sat cross-legged on a table in the mess and waited.

Frigate *APS Summoner's* captain had announced an inspection party for a routine check. The crew should assemble in the mess or on the bridge and await further instructions.

More than once, she had judged boarding or even the request to bring a ship about as piracy, but this was an AP ship in an AP system inspecting an AP merchant, so it had to be okay—kind of.

She reached out for emotions.

Basically, the *Easiness of Low Aspiration's* crew had no reason to fear anything. Their registration was okay, their cargo legal, even their latest new crew member hired by the Books and registered, so it should be just routine. Still, she sensed fear, uncertainty, worries, bitterness.

On the other side, from the airlock, came different emotions. Boredom in some, eagerness in others, paired with masked anger—anger in search of a target to vent it on, a dangerous sign.

She knew about that—her instructors had taught her and her fellow officer candidates to spot those signs in their subordinates. The desire to break out of routine, the longing for some thrill, the power a weapon could give to people with an inferiority complex—play strong, gain attention, gain acceptance among their fellow recruits—if those people weren't reined in, they'd cause trouble.

Sadly, she didn't sense emotions of anyone with a desire to draw in the reins in the small boarding party.

She wasn't at all inclined to spread for a painful gangbang, so the next quartercycle would become interesting.

Syreen could feel emotions springing to attention—the two men in combat suits entering the mess radiated interest, desire, lust and hunger upon sight of her.

She smiled and pulled her shirt over her head. "Guys, you can't do it wearing all that armor. The first one undressed can have a go with me first."

Her open invitation caught them off-guard. A gentle mental push sufficed, and they started unlocking their armor.

She had all the time in the world to take off her boots and pants and put her neatly folded clothes aside.

Soon she faced two erect cocks—and she still wasn't interested in sex.

"Jerk off," she commanded, audibly and mentally. While the two men started to rub their members, she ambled up to one of them, stepped behind him, reached around to his balls, and then sank her fangs into his neck.

His lust added a nice taste to his blood.

Go on your knees and suck, she ordered his teammate, in time to prevent her victim from shooting his load all across the floor. That way, she didn't have to clean up.

Next, she made them change position.

You remember my pussy and me sucking your cock, and you had a great time. But you'll only tell your mates after the next jump.

CHAPTER FIFTY-EIGHT

As soon as the inspection team had left, Syreen joined the crew on the bridge — of course refreshed and without blood stains, and appropriately dressed again.

The skipper gave her a worried look. She sensed his sad compassion.

"Are you okay, Syreen? Would you like some rest and privacy? You could have my cabin."

"Thank you, Skipper, but I'm okay. Junior navigation trainee Syreen reporting back to duty, Sir." She mocked a salute with a shake of her hips, remembering how a similar parody had almost earned her a formal reprimand. Only the fact that her superior hadn't been able to suppress his laughter had saved her back then.

It worked again — the entire crew burst out laughing.

"You're bearing it well," Bhannain said. "Okay, we'll leave it at that. You want to do the calculation?"

"My job, Skipper."

"Okay. Go ahead."

Kaname quickly freed his chair. "Have a seat."

She wouldn't have needed it, but accepted his offer anyway and started by calling up the star map. Sketching the next jump should have been easy, but despite her joke, she soon sensed the men's worries about her return.

It would have been impossible to bear, had she truly been subject to double rape, but for them her abuse was still a fact, and they could hardly stand the thought. In turn, their mix of sadness, shame, guilt, compassion, and frustration distressed her so much that it impaired her concentration.

Syreen couldn't focus on the map before her. She closed her eyes and tried to mute her sense for emotions.

Better.

When she looked at the star map again, she recognized a clear maze of routes. *Yes, this is the obvious route, and that one's less obvious, but works fine.*

She tried both. The computer didn't find anything wrong with either, but judged her second solution as cheaper in terms of wear and significantly faster. It was an easy bet, though, that the *Easiness* had taken the first route until now.

"Here." She turned and looked up to Kaname. "What do you think?"

The pilot leaned over her. "That's the standard route—wasn't hard to figure out, eh? Very good solution on this one. And you found a secondary solution?"

"Yes. Only it's much better."

He pointed at the summary. "Indeed—wow, that's a difference. And where would you—no. Wow. How did you find *that* route?"

"Why? It's not as obvious, okay, but it wasn't hard to see."

"But . . ." He examined her second solution again. "No, indeed. It's easy. But that double star—and that's not really a jump. I didn't know it's at all possible to do such a short hop, but the computer says it works." He walked around the desk, spread his arms, and then looked at her. "But how did you come up with it?"

She didn't avoid his gaze. "I'm a navigator."

He laughed. "That explains everything."

It did, only he couldn't make the connection.

CHAPTER FIFTY-NINE

The first thing Syreen noticed upon their arrival in the Nysa system was the massive presence of warships. They left the main planet — Nysa Three — alone, but were orbiting Nysa Two, Four and Five in scores. A dozen active dreadnaughts, countless battle cruisers, light cruisers, frigates and destroyers, surrounded by swarms of stingships, and of course her plot showed some corvettes, too.

"Is it always that busy here?" she asked Kaname and rose from his lap.

"Lately, yes. As they say, they're after some troublemakers. Just to ensure the safety of interstellar trades, and that's what the inspections are for as well. I'd understand that, but — uh, well."

"Yes, I know. All okay as long as they don't find women." She glanced around. "Not your fault."

The skipper made a face. "It is. I shouldn't have allowed you aboard."

"It was my decision to take that risk. Will there be another inspection upon arrival?"

"The checks for incoming ships are tight, but you needn't fear such abuse again. Moreover, I will file a formal complaint with the port authorities as well as with the guild."

"Leave it."

"Why?"

"There are no witnesses. You didn't watch it happen. It's just my word against theirs, and that will do me no good. Someone might decide to retaliate — or to let me disappear, lest there be damage to the navy's reputation."

He briefly closed his eyes. "Yes. You may have a point there. As you said before, it's you taking the risk, so it's your call. I will not put you in danger, although I don't like the thought of letting them get away with their misdeeds."

"Don't worry about that. One day we'll meet again in a dark alley, and then I'll repay them in kind."

"That's unlikely."

She shrugged. "Yes, but I like the thought anyway." *The thought of sinking my fangs into their throats and tasting their horror before I make them forget.*

"Don't give me that hungry look, like you're about to eat me."

"Oh. Did I? Sorry."

"If looks could kill, those guys are doomed."

"I'll try that."

They gazed at each other for a moment, and then Bhannain broke out into laughter, and the others joined in.

CHAPTER SIXTY

After having passed the immigration check on Nysa Delta Station, Syreen ambled down the central ringwalk contemplating her next steps. She needed more information on Nysa in general, on their government and military in particular, and probably a shuttle dirtside later.

First, she had to come to terms with her arrival. Nobody had attempted to rape her, but the checks had been tight indeed, as Captain Bhannain had promised.

Her *tight check* had included a strip-search including the inspection of all body cavities before the cameras and the entire all-male immigration team, scanning of all her belongings — shorts, shirt, boots, credit stick and tab. A cycles-long interview session with different people asking her the same questions again and again had followed — where she came from, where she would go, her profession, her business on Nysa, why she traveled without luggage, and so on — before her belongings were returned to her.

Nudity didn't mean anything to her, but the process had been humiliating in so many other ways that it still rankled inside her. Only the necessity of keeping her beast at bay had allowed her to remain calm and focused — and had spared the immigration team a gory surprise.

Such an incident wouldn't have helped me to remain incognito, she reassured herself. *However, should I run into any of them off-duty, I'll consider his nutritive value. Until then, I should really work on my planning. Starting with where I am now.*

Nysa Delta was spacious, crowded, and poorly

maintained. The walls were speckled and scratched, the floors sticky and dusty, and the air smelled foul and stale. Why? Every Duchy spaceman knew that loose dust, dirt, and grease aboard ships and stations would eventually accumulate in the air regeneration systems, impairing their functionality. Cheap cleaning robots were invented to prevent most of those problems, but she didn't see any.

In contrast, the people frequenting the station obviously put value in tidy, clean clothing as well as bodily hygiene. If she wanted to remain inconspicuous, she had to adapt. After all, she couldn't keep up her *ignore me*-aura forever.

Before she procured a more decent set of garments, she had to make up her mind about which role to play. The Duchy officer was out of the question. For interstellar tourism, her funds were too tight. For a local, she knew too little about Nysa or even the Association as a whole.

The only role she could believably play was the merchant crew member—after she had arrived as junior navigation trainee, she might as well be one for the duration of her stay. With the significant bonuses from her last two hires, she could afford a trip down to the surface, and her youth sufficiently gave her curiosity a reason to do so.

Moreover, neutral merchant uniforms were the easiest attire to find on the station, and the most affordable. She only had to decide on color and cut, and opted for black uniform leggings with a jacket that the shopkeeper called *cadet gray*—with a blueish hint.

She could keep her shirt, while the pockets left enough room for her folded shorts and the tab, and the entire attire blended nicely in with all the other station visitors. So equipped, she followed a flock of other merchants through a pub door.

CHAPTER SIXTY-ONE

The pub itself was sticky in more than one regard. The air conditioner fought a futile battle against the smells of food, drinks and people. The noise of numerous heated conversations condensed into a tough syrup, and a tsunami of emotions came with them. Still, Syreen could easily navigate her way past the people near the bar and approach the tables in the back.

Quite a few curious glances followed her, some accompanied by rather lewd emotions, others with a more friendly taste. As there were no free tables, she approached an empty chair at one with more friendly patrons. "May I?"

"Sure." The bearded man briefly waved his hand. "You're welcome."

"I'm Syreen."

"John. I'm an engineer on the *Hoboken*. These are Ken, our pilot, Doug, cargo master, and there you got Miku, Ras and Han of the *Kobayashi*." He pointed around the nodding people. "What are you doing? What's a young woman doing in space?"

"I was junior navigation trainee on the *Easiness of Low Aspiration*. I'm looking for another hire, but haven't made up my mind yet."

Ken leaned forward. "Navigation? Aren't you too young for that job yet?"

"I wasn't aware that there's an age requirement for programming a navigation computer."

John laughed. "She's got you there!"

Ken smiled. "Nah, but you need experience. Too many ships are lost between the stars."

"Not those I traveled with," she said.

John uttered another laughter. "Scored again!"

"Go easy with her," Ras chimed in. "She's a trainee. That means there's always an experienced pilot to supervise her. Right, Syreen?"

"Right, Ras. He's doing his calculations and I'm doing mine, and then we compare and propose the best solution to the skipper."

"Have you already won once?"

"Always." She enjoyed his puzzled face. This statement required an explanation, though, but she wouldn't give herself away. "No, really. Perhaps it's the routine. He picks a route that's always worked fine and won't bother to fiddle with the parameters much. I'm fresh and supposed to learn, so I create a route from scratch—often the same as his—and try to fine-tune it as much as possible. The results were often a notch better."

Now Ken and Ras nodded knowingly.

"Makes sense," Ras said. "It's usually not worth the effort, but for a trainee that's a good exercise."

Not worth the effort? You have no clue.

"Okay, so you had good instructors?" Ken asked.

"I think so, yes," Syreen agreed. "Of course, there's only so much instructors can teach. There comes a time when you have to go outside and make your own experiences. That's what I'm doing now."

"And it works out?" Ken glanced at Ras, then back at her.

"Sure. I'm learning a lot, not just about jumping. There's so much you need to know about ports."

"Don't you fear pirates—I mean, as a woman?"

Syreen frowned. "So far, I haven't had trouble with pirates. The last routes seemed to be safe—the skippers didn't bother to ask for escorts. Inspections are different, though."

Now the men around her looked concerned.

Ken asked, "Tough for women?"

"Women are fair game. You better accept that if you want to fly to the stars."

"You mean . . ."

"It's just not called rape because you'd better play along." *Or bite them.*

"Well," John said. "Going to space isn't meant for women."

"Nonsense," Syreen said firmly. "Space isn't dangerous for women. Men are. Moreover, how many members of AP navy are women?"

"Are there any?" John asked back.

Ras nodded. "Sure. When they started their recruitment campaign, they explicitly encouraged women to join the navy, for enlisted ranks as well as for officer careers. If I re-member right, that wasn't all new, but on a larger scale."

"A recruitment campaign?" she asked. "Is it still running?"

"No idea. Want to join?"

Syreen shrugged. "Perhaps it's a better place for a female pilot. I assume crewmates aren't subject to rape. Would be bad for discipline."

CHAPTER SIXTY-TWO

A few mugs of forwine and a hot meal later, Syreen had learned little about her destination—Nysa—but a lot about the Association navy's activities in and around their area of influence. Piracy was on the decline—there were simply too many warships traveling their hunting grounds, and while there were many things Syreen didn't like about the Association—first of all their refusal to declare war appropriately—their policy of firmly and terminally dealing with pirates earned her approval.

With their frequent and unannounced inspections, no merchant ship could expect to hide illegal laser guns away. A merchant with laser guns was a pirate, end of discussion.

"Well, there's one exception, of course," Ken said. "A merchant ship can be re-registered as navy vessel, get a navy transponder signal, and be commanded by a navy officer. It can still carry cargo, but it also can legitimately be armed."

"Why would you do that?" John asked. "With that changed transponder signal, you can't fool anyone. Pirates won't fall for that."

"War zone transports," Ras guessed.

John shook his head. "Such a freighter won't survive a centicycle in a fight with any warship."

"Except against a stingship or two," Syreen objected. "Of course, you'd need a good gunner. At least it might make stingship pilots a bit more reluctant."

Ken smiled at her. "That's what trainees learn?"

"Nah. Experience. You just need precise calculations to hit

167

a stingship. The formulas aren't any more complicated than those for a jump."

"So. But as stingship pilot, you'd be reluctant?"

"Me? No. I wouldn't even hesitate to attack a dreadnaught. Anything else would be cowardice in the face of the enemy."

"Easily said."

John shook his head. "Ken—remember what she's already endured, what she told us before. That was *not* easily done. I doubt you'd muster the same courage. I know I wouldn't."

Ken opened his mouth. Syreen sensed his protest, but she also sensed how it disappeared.

The pilot watched her for a while, and then he said, "No, you're right, John. I can't match her determination. I must believe her. She'd pull that stunt through."

I did. If you knew . . .

"I'm facing a different challenge now, though," she said. "I want to visit Nysa, and I have no clue what I need to travel dirtside—or what to see there. Do you have any ideas?"

"Going down is no deal," Ras said. "Follow the signs for the planetary shuttle service, buy a ticket, check in, and travel."

"Aren't there immigration checks?"

"Sure, but those go easy."

I've heard that before. Oh well.

"About what to see—if you can afford it, you really should check Majesty Falls. You never saw so much water in motion."

They all agreed on that. From then on, they disagreed on some items, but Syreen duly took notes on her tab.

CHAPTER SIXTY-THREE

Syreen tried to steel herself for the expected *easy* immigration checks. Again, she couldn't dare to use her special skills before the cameras, neither the bite nor mental commands. Someone could wonder why the officers didn't have their fun with just this pretty young woman.

Chickening out was out of the question. *Fleet won't give up, and I'm all that's left of Fleet.*

But when she stood in front of the immigration desk and the officer asked her to enter cabin seven for inspection, she found herself close to tears. *There's only so much I can bear. Oh fate, let me be strong one more time.*

A gray-haired woman closed the door of cabin seven behind her, and then held her arm. "Child, you're shaking. What's up with you?"

"N-nothing." She straightened herself and glanced at the pale cabin walls. She was alone with the other woman.

"Your name is just Syreen? No second name?"

She nodded.

"Okay. Sorry for the inconvenience, but we must protect our world against parasites. Would you please remove your clothes for the inspection? Meanwhile, I'll check your arrival protocol."

While Syreen took off her new uniform, the immigration officer operated her pad, shook her head, tapped, brushed, shook her head again.

Waiting in her birthday suit, Syreen tried not to think of the next step. She failed, and again trembled.

The older woman noticed her. "Are you feeling cold? We'll be through with this in no time. Let me see your ears."

She had a little stick to light inside the ear. "Okay, other side. Thank you, you're fine. Now please turn around, lean forward and pull your butt cheeks apart."

The officer's matter-of-fact approach helped a little, but the trembling didn't stop.

"Thanks again. I'm sorry, but I must check your vagina, too. Can you open it for me, or should I use a speculum?"

A tear dropped on the floor, and Syreen pulled her labia apart.

"That's it. Let go, get up—you can put your clothes on again. Hey—you're crying?" The woman cocked her head. "There's something odd about your arrival check. There's no imagery. Girl, tell me what happened."

Syreen grabbed her uniform leggings and shook her head. "Nothing."

"Ratshit." The officer shook her tab. "I've got the protocol here, and the duty roster. You've been inspected upon arrival, but there was no female officer on duty. So who did the inspection?"

Syreen looked down, balancing on one foot while pulling the leggings over her other leg. "All of them."

"All. Girl, you needn't tell me more. I'm sorry for you. This is not what visitors to Nysa should find. It's against the regulations, and they will pay for it." She shook her head. "Poor girl."

Syreen fought with her balance. The officer steadied her, and she could pull her leggings over the second leg and up. "Thank you. I don't want to follow up on this."

"Bah. You don't have to. I will follow up. Either they didn't inspect you, although the protocol says they did—and you know they did—or they inspected you without calling a female officer in. Either is against the regulations. But doing so with the cameras switched off is a major offense—and a most stupid thing to do, because whatever they did, without strong evidence in their favor, they will be sentenced for what they *could* have done. And my inspection proves you're no virgin anymore. You needn't worry about revenge—they'll most likely be taken to Nysa Four, have their balls cut off, and then sent to mining work."

"Uh." Now Syreen shivered for the thought.

The officer laughed. "About the balls—I meant that figuratively, but they'll go to the mines anyway. Meanwhile, you're okay. Have a nice stay on Nysa."

CHAPTER SIXTY-FOUR

Buckled to her seat inside the big shuttle, Syreen wondered which had been worse. The inspection? Short, matter-of-factly, for acceptable reasons, but still highly humiliating. Why couldn't it be left to a machine? Did they subject rich tourists to the same kind of inspection? Or was the ease with which she had been dismissed worse? *Oh, you were abused? Don't worry, I'll file a charge, thank you, now make room for the next patron.*

No. The worst about it was that the women were no better than the men. Rude, ruthless, hidden behind a shallow façade of mocked friendly politeness.

She'd have sensed the officer's compassion, had there been any. But she had sensed nothing, except for a glimpse of dismay on the other inspection team's failure to comply with regulations. Their victim didn't count.

There had to be something fundamentally wrong with this society. Their male officers could take what they wanted, their navy could act as desired without the legitimation of a declaration of war, navy crew again could just take without fear for disciplinary retaliation. Who guided them, who demonstrated values to the Nysa people? And what kind of values? Jungle law, where the strongest ruled?

She had seen jungle law at work on Appalahoo. The real law — eat or be eaten. She had adapted to it, and used it to her advantage. If Nysa worked by this ruleset, she knew how to act.

Once on the ground and through the checks, she'd feed her

beast.

The idea made her smile, and her smile made the passenger on the next seat reconsider his intentions. His emotions changed from curious anticipation to wariness.

In a way, she could relate to all these emotions. On her journey to Nysa, she had been curious about what she'd find, too, and she had to admit a certain level of anticipation. Both still applied now that she was going dirtside. Her recent experience with AP officials hadn't changed that, but in addition had nurtured her own wariness. This nation was dangerous for young female foreigners, and not just for spies.

In turn, she was dangerous, too. No one could prepare the locals for what would come upon them.

You started a war on the Duchy? You didn't know, but you also started a war on the People. Now learn what that means. Poor bastards.

CHAPTER SIXTY-FIVE

After leaving the shuttle port — without any new humiliating checks — Syreen headed straight for one of the numerous tour operator offices. If she could find any tour including a visit around Nysa's capital, she'd be another step closer to her mission goal.

Nysa's blueish sun soon felt hot on the unprotected parts of her skin, so she was glad to leave the open sky behind her.

A clerk sitting at a desk looked up. "Welcome to Nysa. What can I do for you — oh, you're not used to our sun, are you?"

"I'm not at all used to open skies."

"Ah, you're a spacer? You should wear a hat, and perhaps take a sunscreen pill. The sun can be hazardous to your skin."

"I'll do that. Thank you."

"You're welcome."

"Okay — I just arrived on Nysa. I don't want to waste any time finding my way around. You have packaged tours?"

"Of course."

Syreen spent the next quartercycle browsing the local tour operators' offers and discussing pros and cons with the clerk. She finally decided on a tour that wouldn't stretch her budget too much, departing the next morning, took note of recommendations on tourist traps and solid businesses, an affordable bed-and-breakfast, coincidentally run by the clerk's aunt, and memorized directions to a hat shop and a drugstore.

Thus prepared, she ventured outside under the open sky and burning sunlight again. She had to bear it for another cycle until sunset—time to be put to good use.

She bought a wide-brimmed hat, which added much to her comfort. The sunscreen pills helped again—after a brief consultation with the drugstore keeper, she took two, and the burning feeling faded soon.

Only now did she find leisure to inhale the unfamiliar smells of another new planet, listen to its sounds, feel the natural gravity of its large mass and the draft of air around her skin, and sense the locals' emotional aura.

Her basic impression was its density—Nysa's capital had about ten million inhabitants, crammed into a tight saddle between steep mountains toward both poles and large oceans around the equator. Buildings dug deep into the mountains or crawled up their flanks, and a large part of public life took place on rooftops and bridges.

Publicly available data had told her that the shuttle port was located on a rocky ledge, a third of the way up the mountain. It was quite another orbit to see the port, the mountain, the city below, and the sea with her own eyes.

Syreen was momentarily amazed. Maybe that was why she didn't notice the men approaching her before it was too late—before she noticed the little sting in her neck, felt her legs give in and her vision fade . . .

PART THREE—TORTURE

CHAPTER SIXTY-SIX

There was noise, the distant shuffling of fabric on fabric. There were awful smells — sweat, urine, sanitizer. There was a heavy pull at Syreen's wrists, above her head, and it hurt. Her bare feet touched the wet ground, spread apart, and her legs didn't support her weight. Yet. Would they, if she tried?

When she tried, she felt the weakness in her legs, but the relief to her wrists, arms, and shoulders was too good to give in again.

What happened to me?

There were those men — and then I was gone. They must have drugged me. Who? And why?

Insufficient data. I must be patient and wait for my opportunity.

Next, there was light, blinding her through closed lids. It took her a moment to adapt, and then she opened her eyes to examine her surroundings.

She saw indirectly lit gray walls, square, six legs from corner to corner, gray ceiling, and gray floor, the latter with a wet puddle between her feet. Manacles around her ankles were chained to rings in the floor, and her wrists were similarly chained to rings in the ceiling. By turning her head, she could spot a doorframe. Other than that, the room was empty.

This was about to change, as she sensed a strong emotional presence approaching — it made her duck away mentally, close her mind against the *gooey* feeling.

After a sudden rush of air, the noise of a sliding door

behind her, and then of footsteps, a tall man appeared in Syreen's field of vision, his toned body clad in a white AP uniform with the five stars of an admiral on its shoulders, wearing his long black hair in two plaits. His bright green eyes reminded her much of her own.

She couldn't estimate his age. His skin looked too smooth for an aged man, with no wrinkles or signs of a beard, while his edgy face betrayed the initial juvenile expression.

"Thank you for saving us a lot of effort to find you, Lieutenant Syreen," he started in a deep baritone and grinned at her surprise. "You didn't really think you could come here and remain unseen?"

With spread arms, he walked around her, stopped behind her, then ambled on and came into her sight again. "The computer checks we set up on your person were primarily meant to find you somewhere closer to your Duchy, but it was no extra effort for our programmers to deploy them everywhere within our reach. So, when a woman of the right size, right eye color, and right name showed up on Nysa Delta Station, we were alerted. When she accepted the rough immigration check without protest, we knew what to make of it."

He stepped closer, and she could smell his clean breath. "I'm quite curious how you managed to escape us on Eiffel. That's where the *Easiness of Low Aspiration* came from, didn't it?"

Did I? Or didn't the news reach you yet?

"You know, our secret services aren't dense. You did a good job covering up your escape by blowing up a dreadnaught — and you will tell me how you did it in due time — but of course, our corvette's transponder code could be easily tracked and matched with certain . . . incidents along your route. By the way, a pity you didn't return the ship to us. I might have credited you with just borrowing it instead of stealing it. That would have counted in your favor."

Sure. And its computer would have told you volumes. No way.

"As you may have noticed, you're not in a position to make demands or deny your cooperation, unless you want to make your stay even more uncomfortable than it already is. Sadly, you seem to be accustomed to bearing humiliation, so I may be forced to resort to other means of *instructing* you."

He pointed down between her feet. "Before we begin, let me establish a few rules. First, you will only do as you're told. You will not walk on your own, speak unprompted, or shed your bodily waste without order. Second, failing to follow the rules will subject you to punishment. Third, you will answer my questions fully and truthfully — again, failing to do so won't do you any good. Fourth, you will call me *master*. Do you understand?"

Go and fuck yourself, she thought. But defiance wouldn't help her, she had to play along. "Yes, *master.*"

"Good girl." Again, he pointed down. "This time, I will leave your misbehavior unpunished, as you were unconscious. This must not happen again. I will have it cleaned up before we continue."

Next, he left her.

Bastard.

CHAPTER SIXTY-SEVEN

The cleaner came, cleaned, and left.

Syreen was left alone with her thoughts and the smell of sweat and more sanitizer.

Nude, chained in uncomfortable position, and not allowed to pee – that's how you plan to get my cooperation? You should not get your throat into reach of my fangs.

There had been something disturbing about his mental presence. As long as she couldn't sort it out, she wouldn't try her own mental powers on him—she'd better play the ordinary Duchy lieutenant as long as possible. Her skills might give her an advantage only once, and she'd need that on her escape.

Until then, she might gather more information out of her *master*, talkative as he was. After all, he had spared her a lot of effort—unveiling his existence, finding his lair, intruding it, making him talk with her. Why should she spoil it all now by angering him?

Okay, there were a few potential reasons. The manacles around her wrists chafed, her shoulder joints hurt, her arms were pure pins and needles, his manners left much to ask for, and she'd like to take a shower.

But she was still Fleet, and Fleet wouldn't give up.

The rush of air from the opening door was the only warning about his reappearance. Obviously, Syreen had managed well to mute her senses.

"So. Cleaned up again. Are you willing to answer my

questions now, Lieutenant Syreen?"

"Yes, master."

"Very well. Tell me more about yourself."

"I am Lieutenant Syreen of Duchy Fleet, acting Fleet Commander in Charge. Until the raid on the Duchy, I was a skirmisher pilot, and I was one of the best. That's the reason I survived the Association's initial attack wave. When I found myself to be the last survivor, field-promoted to fleet commander, and my base destroyed, I opted for a tactical retreat. My best option seemed to be hiding aboard one of the big ships, so I abandoned my skirmisher before it was shot and approached a dreadnaught in my evac suit."

"In your *evac suit?*"

"Yes, master. Not that I had many options left. Next, I boarded the dreadnaught through a maintenance hatch."

"You weren't smashed on impact?"

"No, master. I forgot to mention my seat, equipped with rockets for deceleration."

"Well. You were aboard. Weren't there guards?"

"Yes, master. Initially, I hid away from them. Then I stole an AP pilot uniform. Disguised as a recently arrived pilot, I could persuade an admiral to issue me a new order, with which I then procured the corvette."

He smiled. "You mean you had an order to take that ship?"

"Yes, master. Due to that order, I could leave the Duchy system unchallenged."

"That, and the fact the dreadnaught blew up shortly after your departure."

"Yes, master."

"Just coincidentally."

Syreen couldn't know what intel he had, so she had to stay close to the truth.

"No, master. I must admit my involvement in that mishap. It seems that a dreadnaught reactor won't behave well if all its safeties are shut down."

"We guessed that much, but it shouldn't be possible anyway. Once you shut a safety down, another will start up."

"Unless it's put to extended maintenance, master. Which I did with all safeties."

He stared at her face, at her thighs, and at her face again. "So that's how you did it. You're very clever."

"Yes, master—no, master. If I were, I wouldn't be here." She shook her wrists. The chains clinked.

"That wasn't a question," he said absently and ambled around her. Next, she felt a rush of air, a sting of pain on her buttocks, and heard the echo of a loud smack.

"Ouch!"

He returned to her front and held up a flexible whip she hadn't noticed before. "You're not supposed to speak unasked for."

She kept her mouth shut and nodded while the slowly fading pain pulsed through her rear.

"Well. Let's recap your journey now. What was your next stop?"

"Kyris, master."

The whip in his hand twitched.

She quickly added, "It took me three jumps to get there, and after the second, I met a merchant under pirate attack. The pirate requested surrender."

"But you refused?"

"Yes, master. Or, put differently, I shot his ship as my message of refusal. Thereafter, he surrendered to the merchant crew."

"I heard about that kill. I didn't know our corvettes could do such precise shots."

Was that a question? No.

Her host nodded. "How did you manage it, anyway?"

"I had to do some additional calculations, master. The

formulas are there in every ship computer, but used to calculate intrasystem ship courses. With little modifications, they can be used to calculate laser shots, too."

"Little modifications, eh? I guess you used these modifications again at Brannock, didn't you?"

"I did, master."

"Can you explain them?"

"Yes, master. The standard formulas are kept simple for ease of use. After replacing the approximations with the real differential equations, you only need to have a set of equations for your own ship, another for the target, and a third for the pulse cannon shot, which is traveling at light speed. After that, you can find a set of solutions—along the timeline—where the shot hits the target, and you just have to pick one."

"That easy, eh? I think you're mocking me."

"It's not easy, master. The formula sets are complicated, as they must allow for acceleration and three-dimensional movements. However, your evidence supports my statement, as I did score."

He slowly nodded. "That is true. Okay, I will check that with my experts. In the meantime, make yourself comfortable."

Laughing, he walked away, leaving her hanging from her chains.

CHAPTER SIXTY-EIGHT

After what felt like a tencycle to Syreen, but probably wasn't more than a cycle, her interrogator — master — returned.

"Okay, girl," he said and clapped his hands. "I've asked one of my math experts, and he said it could be done — there might be just a few of his fellow experts who might be able to copy your method. Surely neither of our officers could. So how can a mere lieutenant handle such complex math?"

"I've been the best in my class, master. I would say the same feat was beyond most of my dead wingmates, agreed, but I could demonstrate it any time — where I must admit I didn't do it by heart. I need to write the formulas down, and for doing the actual number crunching, I need a computer."

He nodded. "That's about what my expert said. Okay, I'll buy that for now. Let me address another interesting topic — how did you manage to find that lost system?"

Should she deny knowing about it? No. The buoy she had left there — which the first flotilla hadn't found the time to kill — could be tracked back to Kyris, where she had bought it. The Association spies couldn't have missed that.

A sudden smack at her upper leg made her wince.

"You're supposed to answer without delay."

"I am Syreen, Duchy Fleet lieutenant, *master*. I cannot tell about Duchy military secrets."

"Are you ready to suffer the consequences, Lieutenant?"

"No, master, but I will not break my oath." *And I can bear a few smacks.*

Syreen was right, and she was terribly wrong. He started with a few firm smacks on her buttocks. She moaned, but refused to answer his question.

Next, he smacked her calves. It hurt, but wouldn't make her reconsider.

I'm Fleet. I won't surrender to a few smacks.

Ouch.

Or to a few more.

"So." He walked around her once, twice, a third time. She could almost taste the malice he radiated. Where would he hit next?

Entirely unexpected came the sudden mental pressure assaulting her defenses.

Obey, he demanded. *Answer me.*

She clenched her teeth and fought to keep him out of her head. Her surprise had to stand back.

"Fascinating," he commented. "This is new."

Answer me.

She focused on her hurting skin instead.

Finally, he shrugged. "It won't matter. You will soon wish you'd answered me when you could."

This announcement didn't sound promising at all, but she was still marveling at her host's mental skills. He had tried to influence her!

He left without another comment.

In a galaxy so large, I couldn't expect to remain the only one. To find another talented person here, of all places, strikes me as odd, though. However, with such abilities it's no wonder he's in charge.

Which means he's the one behind the search for the relic.

Which means he knows of the Forgotten People.

Which in turn most likely means he's one of them — of us.

Shouldn't we be allies, then?

Considering my current situation, that could help me, but it would mean breaking my Fleet oath.

Considering my current situation, would I want to ally with him? With a man who chains prisoners to the ceiling and flogs them?

Would I want to take sides with a man who so ruthlessly kills civilians by the score, without warning, without declaration of war? Would I want Assiduous taking sides with him? I answered that question before — no, I wouldn't. That he might be of the People doesn't change a thing. He's a rogue, like I am, but he's a bastard rogue. He must not learn what I know. I'd rather die.

Which might happen.

CHAPTER SIXTY-NINE

Again, there was a draft when the door opened, but this time, the footsteps sounded different. Next, a stocky man stepped before Syreen.

He wore nothing but very tight-fitting shorts, a muscle shirt and a small bag.

"Good evening, my lady. I am Paolo, your drill instructor. During the next cycles, I will demonstrate you all the different flavors of pain your body is able to recognize. The purpose is, of course, to instruct you in proper submission to the master's queries. You need not bother to make any offers to me. I will not listen to answers or pleas, but only to your screams, and I will not pause or stop my instructions before completion."

She believed him.

"Just for the records," she said anyway. "I'm a Duchy officer and may claim appropriate treatment. Failing to do so may cause repercussions not only for the wrongdoer but also his nation, if performed under order. I assume you know the relevant regulations."

"Nothing you say will have any effect on my actions, but babble on as you like as long as you can."

Yes. The more he talked, the more she could learn about him and this *master,* and perhaps about a way out of her current unfavorable situation.

"Do you like what you do?"

"It doesn't matter what I like to do. I'm doing as the master commands, and you'll learn that, too. I'd really appreciate if you'd profit from my instructions, though. I don't like to

187

waste my efforts for nothing, you know?"

"That's what my instructors said, too."

"So you'll understand that you have to learn." He put down his bag, leaned down, and opened it.

"I already learned that I must obey my superiors, do my duties, and keep my oath. What the master requests is the opposite."

Paolo rose, holding a small silver hammer in his hand. "What you must learn is this — there is no superior for you but the master. Your only duty is to obey him, and before him, any oaths are void."

He ambled around her. Next, she felt a stinging pain at her right elbow when his hammer hit her funny bone, and gasped. Before she could recover from her surprise, he hit her left elbow, and then her knee, the other — and again.

Her vision blurred under a veil of tears, and she couldn't help but moan with every hit. *Stop! Please!*

Paolo paused only for a moment, and then he went on.

Syreen tore at her chains, but in vain. Her tormentor didn't even comment on her attempts. Methodically, he started to hit her ankles. When she thought it couldn't become worse, Paolo began to hammer her toenails.

CHAPTER SEVENTY

Syreen's tears had joined to form a new puddle on the floor. Her entire body hurt from Paolo's hammer, his whip, his pinchers, and the club, which he all had methodically applied to almost every region of her body.

The bruises would take a while to turn dark, Paolo had assured her, but she could be sure they'd show up in time for the master's next visit, together with the welts from her flogging. Meanwhile, she should contemplate her pain in solitude.

She looked forward to that visit. Perhaps the sight of her mistreated body could incite the master to some mercy and make him stop her treatment.

Meanwhile she focused on her slowly fading pain. At first, she had tried to fancy different treatments she'd apply to Paolo, should he be careless enough to unchain her. She hadn't been able to keep her mind focused. Instead, her thoughts circled around the mutilations he'd done to her body. She'd never be pretty to look at again.

Her mental defenses were down for sure. After his first few hits, she had no longer been able to blind out Paolo's emotions. He didn't feel happy or satisfied by his actions, but rather angry at her. Why? Because of her defiance? In any case, his feelings toward her hadn't made her time any more comfortable.

When she sensed Paolo's approach—and not the master's—her heart sank. Why him again?

He didn't bring good news, that much she could tell. When

he entered and wordlessly dropped his small bag before her, and she could sense his dismay, she expected the worst.

She got even worse.

This time, red and black veils fought for dominance over her vision. The smell of her own scorched flesh caused her nausea, and her nail-less feet could hardly bear her weight anymore.

When he raised some small, sharp item toward her shoulder, she whispered, "No, please." *Wait.*

Paolo paused. "The master demands visible proof of my work. I must mark you in every way. I will take just some tiny bits of your skin."

He did.

Syreen woke from a slap at her cheek. Compared to what she had taken before, it felt like a tickle. Nevertheless, her cheek felt hot.

No more. I can't bear any more!

"I might have overdone it a bit, eh?" Paolo said. "Seemingly, you can't bear any more of this kind. But remember, as long as you won't cooperate, I must continue my instructions."

The misty haze around her mind cleared.

So I can give commands as long as they don't contradict the master's orders?

"What's next? The pain a broken leg can inflict? You might accidentally lean down on it, causing yourself the sweetest agony, plus it increases the terrible strain on your arms. Would be interesting, don't you agree? Or, perhaps I'll save that for later. We don't want you to faint again yet, do we?"

We'll save that for later.

When he licked his lips, an idea occurred to her.

She cocked her head. "The worst pain I ever felt was when I accidentally broke a tooth. You might want to check that."

Come close and have a look.

"You're begging for it? You must be insane." Paolo stepped up to her, almost touching her charred tits. "But it's an outstandingly good idea. Perhaps I should pull one? Let me see."

Closer.

Then she started choking and rolling her eyes, rattled her wrist chains, and squealed.

Untie me, or I'll suffocate.

"Wait, I'll release you!" Paolo made a gesture toward the wall behind her.

Her arms came free, flailed wildly, searching for support. She leaned forward, right into Paolo.

He caught her. "Gotcha, girl."

Gotcha, bastard.

Her fangs sank into his neck, tasting power.

Syreen felt light, relieved of pain, relieved of her corporeal self — new strength flowed through her mind, expanded her senses, washed away her sorrows.

Distant stars sang their melodies — to Syreen their songs were like gentle caresses, soothing her troubled soul, easing the damage her tormentor had done to her mind.

Couldn't it remain so? *No. I must get out of here.*

When her physical awareness returned, she felt better than expected. She let the drained body drop to the floor and glanced at her feet. The chains around her ankles had opened, too.

The skin at her feet should be chafed and red — instead, it looked pale and even. Her toes no longer hurt, were no longer red, and showed newly grown toenails. She raised one hand before her eyes — the same.

The burns, the bruises, the cut-away part of skin, all were healed. She was whole, and Paolo was dead. For him, she felt no remorse. He had been the *master's* tool, but a willing tool — she had sensed no trace of pity in him, not once. Not even in the end, when he had shared her pain.

His scalpel, his worst tool of torture, now had to serve her. She couldn't leave a partially blood-drained, dead body with no visible injuries lying around. She had to cut his throat and make sure he'd spill the little rest of his blood on the floor.

There was no way to pocket the tool, nor Paolo's ID.

What next?

SitOps. Situation — naked, alone, in the enemy's lair, but healthy, replenished, with sound body and mind. Really? Opposition — large in numbers, strong in mental power, knowing my name, rank, and looks. Location — unknown. No, that's crap. How can a Navigator *not know her location?*

She closed her eyes and listened to the stars' songs. Still amazed by this unusual experience, she nevertheless focused on Nysa singing to her planets.

Fourth planet, not the third? So these bastards had me unconscious for long enough to ship me off planet. I'd better avoid another such shot.

Options — I could resist the master once, but could I overcome him? No — I cannot risk such a confrontation without backup. So I must abort the mission and withdraw. But how?

Insufficient data. I must explore.

CHAPTER SEVENTY-ONE

Syreen was quite aware that her naked body wouldn't allow her to blend in with the mostly military personnel on Nysa Four, but as long as she could command passersby to ignore her presence, she remained unmolested.

She couldn't command cameras and other surveillance equipment to ignore her, but among those, only cameras were likely to pick up her lack of wardrobe, and cameras were rare. Most doors and hatches depended on motion or infrared sensors, and those were oblivious to her looks. As long as Paolo's ID tag worked, she didn't worry.

A young navy officer almost ran into her after coming around a corner in a less frequented part of the complex. He was about her size, and that determined his fate.

She cut her mental command, enjoyed his stare at her naked body, and then his terror upon the sight of her fangs before she bit him.

I'm a Navigator and may claim appropriate treatment. Failing to do so may cause repercussions not only for the wrongdoer. You're a willing part of a system that assaulted my home world, and you're a legitimate military target.

Yeah, I'm pissed. Guess why.

Syreen's body was healed and her mind somewhat soothed, but she hadn't forgotten how it felt to be beaten up, flogged, and cut. She'd have felt no remorse for paying in kind—and yet, her victim died painlessly after having come inside her. After all, eventual investigators should find a good reason for his nudity.

She took boots, cap, trousers, shirt, and jacket for her own dress. Only then did she cut his throat.

His underwear and Paolo's broken ID tag went into different ventilation ducts some hundred legs distant from the crime scene.

Now she was playing Captain Ishtar Gryf, former Ishtvan, of the Associated Planets Navy. Sadly, or luckily, he didn't seem to be pilot. Sadly, because she could have tried to steal another corvette. Luckily, because that was what she'd check first if she were in her enemy's boots.

In fact, she wore her enemy's boots now.

CHAPTER SEVENTY-TWO

Syreen quickly discarded the idea of picking up another mock-up mission order. Instead, she approached a navy community center and listened to the conversations of others. Had they already learned about the Duchy spy, or about her escape?

She couldn't tell for sure, but nobody mentioned such a topic.

Wearing uniform required much less mental effort to make potential troublemakers ignore her. After all, most officers weren't looking for a slender female navy officer with short black hair and bright green eyes. Enlisted personnel wouldn't approach her unprompted, and noncoms who had no business with her wouldn't risk being assigned with undesired tasks for appearing unoccupied. This was in no way different from the Duchy.

When a small group of officers led by a one-star rear admiral mentioned their imminent departure, she casually ambled up to their table and joined them.

"Hello, Sirs. I'm Ishtar. The master ordered me to join you on your mission." *And the master ordered you to take me along without questions.*

The admiral's gaze seemed to pass through her. "Of course. Welcome to my crew. I'm Admiral Ersan Tas of the ninety-seventh expeditionary corps, and my flagship is the *Oppression*. This is my Flag Captain Marcelo Munoz. His adjutant will take care of your luggage and accommodation aboard."

She nodded at Munoz. "No luggage, Sir, and I don't want to cause any inconvenience. Just a bunk, and I'm fine. I will in no way interfere with your line of command, but of course, I'm ready to bear my share of daily duties. I'm qualified as a communications operator or as a navigator."

Munoz' face lit up. "That's good to hear. We're always short of qualified staff."

Which navy isn't?

He went on, "If it doesn't bother you to assume some lieutenant grade duties . . ."

"Of course not. Beats idling around, doesn't it?"

She sensed his reservations change toward acceptance. He'd never question his *master's* orders, nor could he question her mental commands, but he didn't have to like either of them. By volunteering for footwork, she had won him over.

The admiral nodded approvingly. He radiated positive emotions, too.

Once aboard the *Oppression*, she should be able to leave the Nysa system undetected. By volunteering for navigation and other bridge crew duties, she'd be among the first to learn about their destination—or approaching trouble like inspections.

The most immediate problem she'd face was that she might grow to actually like the AP people she'd be traveling with, which would later make fighting them harder. However, that was a jump she'd calculate once it was due.

For now, she cast a smile all around, and was repaid in kind.

The subtle method of influencing works better. They aren't even aware of their strings being pulled. Had you tried the same with me, I'd be in your bed now, master bastard.

To be continued . . .

YOU MAY ALSO ENJOY THE FOLLOWING FROM EXTASY BOOKS INC:

Time of Wonders
Valerie J. Long

Excerpt

I am a Navigator. As far as I know, I'm the last surviving female of my People, the only one capable of controlling a living ship. I know, because I found one.

When I listen, I hear the songs the stars are singing to their planets. I hear their lonesome, never answered lament. Their songs guide me through space, let me find the smoothest way through hyperspace.

My enemies are score, and their master is of my People, too. He is searching for an ancient relic to give him power over a living ship. He is a male, though, and thus will never command. The relic he needs is a female Navigator—that's me, only he doesn't know that yet.

When he caught me, he regarded me as nothing more but a defiant obstacle, a minor nuisance to his plans. He didn't recognize the reason for my mental resilience. He had me tortured in order to break me. He failed.

I control the minds of the lesser races. I make them ignore me or follow my orders. By feeding on their blood, I gain power or heal my injuries. Such are the ways of my People, and such I did to my torturer, before I left my enemy master's lair.

"Captain Gryf?"

That's me, Captain Ishtar Gryf. That's the name and role I adopted in order to escape Nysa, the Association's home system. The Association, commanded by their master, sent out ships in search for the relic. They came to my home world, the Duchy, and wiped out our fleet, our orbital stations, our planetary defenses, and every civilian in their way without declaring war. In my eyes, such counts as piracy, and thus every single member of their forces is fair game for me.

"Yes, Flag Captain?"

"Would you like to assist Ensign Torres with his jump calculations?"

"Of course."

This is a request I can never reject. I'm a Navigator, and navigating is what I do.

Syreen had to be careful not to give herself away. So she walked over to the navigation dashboard on the battle cruiser's spacious bridge and silently watched the ensign entering his parameters. When he was ready and looked up, she gave him an approving nod. There was no flaw in his setup for this easy jump.

However, when he reached for the button to release his five-sigma solution, she said, "Wait."

He turned to her again with a puzzled face. "Captain?"

"There is no flaw in your solution, Ensign. But why didn't you look for possible refinements? There's no pressing need to jump, as we haven't even reached jump speed yet."

"Uh, what refinements, Captain?"

Syreen had to fight with herself not to roll her eyes. What did the Association teach those young officer candidates?

Neither would she teach her tricks to the enemy, nor could she let such an outrageous lack of knowledge about the most elementary procedures stand. "Recall your parameters."

He did.

"Good. Now call up the trims."

"Trims?"

"That scales symbol, top right."

"Oh — sure."

He tapped it, and a new set of controls appeared.

"See? Now you can adjust your solution. The colors tell you where you can expect improvements. Note there may be good reasons not to change certain parameters too much, depending on where you want to go, but you can try and compare several settings. Go ahead."

The candidate started to change settings.

"Note how the colors on the other controls change. Some of your changes will offer you more options, others may narrow down good choices — which means it's an overall tighter solution."

Torres nodded and moved a few sliders, shook his head, reset them and tried others. Only once she insinuated a cough, which quickly made him reset his last change.

Syreen patiently watched him pick three variations, compare them and arrive at one new solution.

"This is better, I'd say."

This time Syreen nodded. "How much better?"

The ensign checked again and blushed. "Oh. Almost a sigma level."

"So."

"Captain Gryf?" Flag Captain Munoz' demanding voice saved the young man from his embarrassment.

Syreen turned around. "Yes, Sir."

"Are you dissatisfied with Torres' solution?"

"No, Sir. We just arrived at a very good result."

"Submit it. I need to check it myself."

"Yes, Sir." She nudged her pupil, and Torres released the refined solution. "You have it, Sir."

The commandant made a grim face and tapped his panel.

His eyebrows rose, his lips opened to a silent "oh," and then he smiled.

"Six sigma, indeed? Who taught you that, Torres?"

The ensign rose. "Captain Gryf did, Sir."

"In just the past five centicycles?"

"Yes, she did, Sir."

"Remarkable. Ensign, you did an excellent job on this. Captain Gryf, I'm grateful for your lesson. Would you assume command for this transit?"

Syreen smiled. "Yes, Sir."

Munoz returned the smile and rose. "I thought so. Take my seat."

ABOUT THE AUTHOR

I am Valerie J. Long, born in 1963. I live and work in Germany as an IT project manager. I like role playing games, and I like putting my ideas on paper. I like all kinds of Science Fiction and Fantasy, I like music, and I like making you bite your nails off.